The Allure of Deception in Romantic Mysteries

D. Henry

Dedication

To the enthusiasts of intrigue and the lovers of suspense,

In the realm of fiction, where reality bends and twists, I think there is a particular subgenre that captures the heart and mind like no other. It is a dance between love and deception, a puzzle that beckons to be solved, a journey that seems to have the potential for both passion and peril.

This dedication is for those who have crafted tales of intrigue, where the lines between truth and falsehood blur and where the pursuit of love is intertwined with the unraveling of a mystery. It is for the authors who have painted vivid worlds filled with captivating characters, where every glance holds a secret, and every word carries a double meaning.

To the readers who have been captivated by the twists and turns of these stories, who have stayed up late into the night to discover the truth, and who have fallen in love with the flawed heroes and heroines - this dedication is for you.

Let us celebrate *The Allure of Deception in Romantic Mysteries*, the thrill of the chase, the satisfaction of solving the puzzle, and the power of love that seems to triumph over all.

Acknowledgment

I would like to express special thanks to Logan Walsh and his team at NY Book Publishers for their contribution to the publishing of my book. Special thanks to my daughters for their motivation. Never give up on your dreams, be resilient and stay in the race. We are all blessed with unique gifts, and we all must preserve to execute them no matter what curves life throws at us.

About the Author

In the vibrant heart of a parish in Jamaica, a young Dianna Henry began her journey, one marked by resilience, passion, and an unyielding love for storytelling. From the bustling streets of her hometown to the quiet corners of classrooms, Dianna's life has been a tapestry of diverse experiences and profound connections.

A dedicated teacher for thirteen years, Dianna imparted knowledge with the same warmth and empathy she now channels into her writing. Her journey as a mother of four - two by birth, Cyzzannesh and Anjreyev, and two by love, Emmett and Claire - has deepened her understanding of life's complexities and enriched her narrative voice.

In her debut novel, Dianna Henry crafts a tale brimming with heartfelt stories and rich drama. Her characters navigate the intricacies of human emotion and relationships, culminating in an ending that lingers long after the final page is turned. Through her vivid storytelling and authentic voice, Dianna invites readers into a world where love, conflict, and resolution intertwine seamlessly.

Prepare to be captivated by a story that is as heartfelt as it is compelling. Dianna Henry's novel is more than a read; it's an experience that will resonate with you, leaving you eager for more.

Introduction

The Allure of Deception in Romantic Mysteries by Dianna Henry is a fictional story that takes readers on a ride through the complicated life of Holly. Holly is a woman who has come across a load of heartache in her life. Her life seems far from simple - she's loved deeply, faced betrayal, and been let down by people she once trusted. But even after everything that happened to her, she remained gritty to find her way through the pain and discover some strength inside her.

Through Holly's journey, Dianna Henry tries to give the readers a look at the ups and downs of relationships where love and disappointments often go hand in hand. Holly's story tries to present the feeling of being torn between the hope of true love and deceit. The author's storytelling is aimed to take us into Holly's world and make us feel her struggles, her heartbreak, and her moments of strength and bravery. We would watch Holly try to let go of the past, find her own identity, and move forward – although it seems that the shadows still hover close and refuse to let go of her.

With the ideas of love and courage, *The Allure of Deception* is aimed to present more than just a romance. Dianna Henry has penned this fictional world of Holly that's aimed to make us feel every moment right along with her. Her story pulls us into a world of romance and mystery and gives us a peek into the strength it takes to keep going, even when things seem impossible.

This novel is a mix of love, suspense, and emotion that shows how one woman fights her way through love, loss, and things in between.

Table of Contents

Page Left Blank Intentionally

Prologue

Her name is Holly. Her namesake is a green plant with red berries, but Holly has brown skin and caramel-colored eyes. Rooted in nothing but her own strength, she stands tall like a giraffe. Usually, she moves through life with sure, swift strides, but there are days when she stumbles. Today is one of those days, and, ironically, it is her birthday.

Phoenix.

It was just like him to find a way to ruin her *one* special day. Typical. Just like him to force his way back into her life when she thought she'd finally scrubbed herself clean enough to be free of him. By the time she reaches the hospital, his condition has deteriorated sharply. Nurses are forced to physically restrain him with his arms and legs bound to the bed. Even now, in the hallway that smelled like antiseptic, she could hear his voice bouncing off the tiled walls of her memory - like a constant stream of verbal nonsense and half-assembled thought.

These are the ravings of a madman.

'Or…' the cold, practical side of her thinks. *"Maybe it's another lie, another con. Like he's run on you from the very beginning."*

Holly's heart bleeds on the inside. On the outside, she is calm and collected, her eyes warm like stained glass on a Sunday morning, subtly flashing in the sunlight. But inside, she still bleeds. It's not a gush or a stream of red like when she cut her hand wide open on a knife as a child - this bleeding is slow, weeping, intermittent. Holly's heart is a half-healed mass of imperfect incisions, dripping, dripping, dripping, barely held together by will, pressure, and prayers. Sometimes, she isn't even sure she believes in her religion anymore.

Holly's head tilts back to rest against the wall as she closes her eyes. It's four in the morning. Work in a few hours. Children waiting. Her world is a ticking time bomb back home.

She finds it almost funny.

As Holly drifts off, a memory surfaces in her mind. It was of the day Phoenix chose to leave. His smile and laugh were genuine that day, though Holly had been wound so tight that her memories of it now seemed... suspicious. Behind that all-too-ready smile of his are the fangs of a jackal - red-tinged, curved, wide, and inviting. Every one of his promises is a lie.

He's going back to his homeland - sun, sand, surf, and beauty. She doesn't know where he got the money, and at this point, she doesn't care. She just wants him gone, off to play his tricks on someone else, just far away from her.

"In another country, they'll treat me like a king, a millionaire. After all, their currency can't stand up to the US dollar."

On the day he leaves, his suit is crisp and squarely pressed, a dark blue dress shirt flawlessly paired with a white coat and gold tie. He looks every bit the businessman - successful, polished, with all the advantages.

He doesn't look like the devil. There's complexity in him.

He wasn't - he isn't - all bad. But when he is, things get shattered, and punches get thrown. After a year, Holly became quite skilled at hiding bruises with makeup.

It was in the sweltering heat of June when he packed his bags and cleared everything out. Holly came home from work to find the place empty, spotlessly clean, as if he'd never been there.

How does someone throw away a full decade of life? Just like that?

Some questions don't have easy answers.

Holly longs for the protector, provider, lover, and father she once fell in love with. But now, he's none of these - or maybe, she thinks, *he never truly was*. Perhaps he's just a wash of heat haze, a phantasm on the summer wind. All Holly knows is that chasing his false light has led her far from shore. Now, the seas are turbulent, the undertow is relentless, and she's just moments away from drowning.

Chapter 1: Under the Harsh Light

Time has passed. Holly lies awake in bed, sheets rumpled, breath stale. She's surrounded by a clutter of past-due notices and bills, their colors muted in the dim light - white, beige, yellow, and occasionally an angry pink, like flushed cheeks. A sound echoes in her consciousness, a remnant from a dream - loud, insistent. Then:

RINNNNNNNG!

And again:

RINNNNNGGG RIIINNNNNNNNGGG!

It's the phone. She stares at it as if it's a snake. Her impulse is to throw it out the window and curl up into a ball. But life and duty won't let her.

She picks up the phone and is greeted by her aunt's voice. It is shrill and incessant, much like the keening wail of a band-saw.

"Holly, listen, child, you need to leave that boy alone. Let him sit and deal with his own foolishness. He's no good to you; he's no good to your children. He's no good to your family. Your girls are in college, they need you, and they come first".

Holly's head throbs as she hangs up the phone, her hand gripping the receiver in a stranglehold. She channels all her energy, all her focus, all her anger into that single clenched fist as if by doing so, she can make everything else feel manageable.

How do you 'manage' the fact that your husband is fucking a fifteen-

year-old?

Holly looks at herself in the mirror now after the shower's naked heat sets her skin glistening. Youth hasn't left her - she realizes this with a smile, the first in a long time, small and fragile like gossamer strands. Her legs are lithe and supple, and her skin is taut and firm. The child - because that's what the *girl* was… a child - had darker skin and a younger body. But she isn't half the woman Holly is.

The phone rings again. Holly doesn't want to answer, but her hand betrays her. It's Pebbie, the landlord. Phoenix is getting worse. Pebbie wants to know if Holly will let him die alone in the hospital. Holly thinks it's none of Pebbie's business, but by the time she hangs up, she's agreed to get his medical report and deliver it in person.

Why do I keep agreeing to things that aren't my concern?

Holly's sobs are long and loud, tears spilling hot and unbidden down her cheeks. She prays for guidance and strength and then crawls back into bed, seeking the comfort of dreams over the harshness of reality.

An indeterminate time later, the phone rings. Again.

Phoenix is apparently dying. Holly books a ticket, informs her boss of a sudden, unplanned family emergency - one that shouldn't take more than five days to resolve. Soon, she's at the airport, greeting a sister she hasn't seen in months. Sometimes, having a medical doctor in the family comes in handy.

The day they met, the sun was blazing hot, and the airport was buzzing with the sound of departures and arrivals and the roar of engines. Holly and her sister wear dresses that ooze with color, fluttering in the wind. Around them, men hustle by - some in suits, others in shorts, futilely trying to escape the midsummer heat. They struggle with heavy suitcases as they make their way to the car and eventually arrive at the hospital just before visiting hours.

Upon entering the hospital, Holly finds fear waiting for her at the entrance like an unwanted suitor. It gets worse the farther in they go, and she's almost tempted to call the whole thing off. But her sister drags her in with a firm, no nonsense grip, and together they make their way to Phoenix's room.

Holly's mind drifts back to her own time in a place like this, only it was Phoenix's hands that put her there. The smell hits her - the sharp, tangy sweetness of sickness, like overripe fruit and under it all, the rough note of synthetic solvents and antiseptics.

She remembers the delirium, the way the smell seemed to creep inside her, threatening to consume the last parts of herself that she'd managed to keep safe - the parts Phoenix hadn't been able to touch. She had sworn never to find herself in a place like this again if she could help it.

"God help me…"

The words slip out with her breath, without conscious thought, as she catches sight of him, sitting curiously on the edge of the bed. When he sees Holly, his face goes blank, as if he's seen a ghost. Slowly, he stammers, "Ho… Ho… Holly"

It's really him. He never could get her name right. Whether it was ineptitude or sheer stubbornness, she was never sure. She looks at him - truly looks at him - for the first time in years.

He's just a man.

What did I ever see in him?

The thought doesn't get a chance to fully form as Holly's sister takes over the conversation, recognizing that Holly is in no state to respond. Phoenix starts pleading with Holly to retrieve his passport from his apartment when, suddenly, a voice says, "Annmarie, this is Ho... Ho... Holly."

Both Holly and her sister look on in amazement as a younger woman enters the room.

"Holly, tell her that we're divorced. Tell her, tell her!"

Holly almost feels like laughing at the utter confusion on the other woman's face. She chuckles softly under her breath.

She doesn't know he's already married. This is a shock to her, too…

For a heartbeat, they all stand there, frozen in disbelief, until Holly's sister breaks the silence.

"Phoenix, since you said you're divorced, do you want to sign the divorce papers now?"

There is another brief moment of silence. And then, Phoenix is moving, sitting up, looking quite well for a sick person.

"Hell no!"

Later, Holly would reflect on the fact that there are levels to every emotion, and everyone's yardstick is different. The girl in that room - this 'Holly' - had gone from a level 3 to a full-blown 12 when Holly and her sister walked in, likely when Phoenix introduced Holly as his wife. Embarrassment is written all over the young woman's face, realizing that Phoenix had promised to marry her when she turned 18. Had she opened her legs to him?

Of course, she had.

***

They were making her come back the next day. After finally securing the report the hospital insisted they needed, after discussing every detail of Phoenix's situation with the on-duty nurse and going back and forth in the hallway with her sister - after all of that, she was still being made to come back.

Holly didn't want to go back. She didn't want to return and be known as the jilted wife, the has-been who once belonged to the dapper man who always spoke so well, who everyone thought was just the nicest—

Bile rose in her throat. The air was still hot, even late at night. She stood on the balcony of her sister's apartment, gripping the railing, staring out at the city's countless pinpricks of light. Sleep did not come easily.

The next day, Nizzy and Holly's sister took their son to school, arranging for his father to pick him up later since the hospital business would likely drag on. When they arrived at the school, Justin asked, "Aunt Holly, can you walk me inside?"

And of course, she said, "Yes, my love, of course," because you can't resist the needs of a child. She walked him in, talked with the teachers, admired his work, praised him, and allowed herself a moment to forget. In that moment, there was no hospital, no heartache, no Phoenix fooling around with some girl barely over the age of consent - just her and her nephew.

Parenting was easy. It was everything else that felt insurmountable.

***

The hospital's parking lot is underground. The air is muggy and thick, the lights harsh and unforgiving. Her sister's car is the only one on their level, so the gray concrete stretches out in an oppressive expanse before her. The joy from her earlier moment with her nephew is long gone and is replaced by a tension as she and her sister step into the elevator, waiting in silence for the doors to open.

The elevator spits them out at the emergency room, and they head to the large intake desk with the report in hand. Holly just wants this to be over. As they wait, her sister asks, "I have to admit, I'm curious why you're here. The doctors are good, the hospital has a solid reputation - hell, I'm a doctor with connections. I don't see why they're denying Phoenix's medication…"

"I'm here now, so let me just leave the paperwork with the doctor so his family can stop accusing me," Holly snapped.

"Give me those stupid papers!" her sister shouts back. Holly tightens her grip on them, and they tug back and forth as the car sways from lane to lane. Their childish behavior almost cost them their lives. They drove the rest of the way in silence until they reached the hospital.

When they arrive at the hospital, Holly's sister is greeted by other doctors. They chat as they approach the ward, only to be interrupted by Phoenix's voice coming from down the corridor. "Where are my pants?" he shouts from his bed. "Come, come and sign my release now! You are my wife - are you afraid?" The doctors immediately call for his medication.

The sisters are stunned, unaware that Phoenix had discharged himself and needed someone to take him home. A security guard restrains Holly from entering the ward, but she quickly slips behind him as the doctors try to calm Phoenix down. The guard restrains him and forces him back onto the bed.

Just as he's about to lie down, Annmarie strolls in wearing tight, washed-out pants and a sleeveless blouse that reveals sagging breasts and a bulging stomach. She's in flip-flops, drawing all eyes to her. Phoenix sees her and suddenly turns toward her, waving his release papers. "Hey baby, here's my release!"

The look on Annmarie's face causes Phoenix's demeanor to quickly shift.

"Damn it, sign this now!"

Her eyes popped open even wider.

"Come on! Look at this hot body. Isn't this what you wanted? Let them know how you like to eat this."

He was about to pull his pants down when the doctors restrained him. By now, a full audience of patients had gathered. One from across the room shouted, "That's what happens to you, licky, licky teenage gal!"

Annmarie turned and fled the hospital, crying. The doctor managed to calm Phoenix down, took his chart, and briefed Holly's sister on his condition.

Holly's sister handed over Phoenix's medical records. The doctors stood there for a brief moment and compared notes and medication types. Holly felt relieved for a moment, but then she remembered she needed to retrieve Phoenix's passport, pants, and a shirt. Her sister thought Holly was extremely mad for wanting to continue these wifely duties. Her sister could not believe what intellectual capacity Holly was functioning on. To placate her sister, Holly was given the benefit of the doubt.

Holly called the landlord for directions, but after several attempts, the sisters kept receiving the wrong instructions. The directions were convoluted: go past the first traffic light, turn left, then right. When you reach a church, look for a mango tree, then go up the hill, and around the corner, turn left, and you'll find a big house at the top of the hill on your right. With such confusing directions, Holly's sister, who was the driver, couldn't make sense of them. When they asked passers-by, they were just as dumb as the person before.

Just as they were about to give up, the landlord called to ask where they were. They sighed heavily and exchanged looks of frustration. "Are people still this dull-witted in this day and age?" they wondered. The landlord couldn't provide clear directions either. Eventually, they directed her to meet them at K&J Bakery back in town. It took another half-hour to reach the bakery, where the crowds were so dense they decided to park by the bank instead.

Five minutes later, the landlord called and asked Holly where she was. She told her they were by the bank. Holly stepped out and stood by the slightly ajar door when a car suddenly pulled up beside them. A cloud of fear enveloped the sisters as four burly men with dark sunglasses jumped out, one with a cigarette hanging from his mouth. Their heads swiveled, scanning the area.

Holly quickly jumped back into the car and closed the door. The men stared at them while Holly and her sister pretended to be busy on their phones, fearing they might be involved in a robbery. The men stood there like a lion on a prowl, communicating with each other through eye gestures. Holly finally decided that she needed to get out and get Phoenix's clothes and passports from this landlord. So, she bravely opened the door and walked toward the bank entrance.

Her phone rang, and Holly answered without hesitation.

"Holly, where are you?" the landlord asked.

Realizing they didn't know each other, Holly replied, "I'm wearing green linen pants."

By the time she provided this detail, the landlord was only an arm's length away. She called out, "Holly!" and they hugged. Holly asked her to lead the way to her villa, and they would follow.

Holly got back into the car and instructed her sister to follow the black Honda SUV. However, her sister put the car in reverse, only to find that the men refused to let them out. A slight fear came over them again, for they were still puzzled as to why they were there and why they refused to let them out. Despite several attempts to maneuver out of the situation, the men remained stationary. Holly's sister kept honking repeatedly and finally, they managed to free themselves from the standoff.

As they drove toward the landlord's villa, they started to discuss what had just happened. *Were they incautious of what they just saw?* They realized the men were likely there to kidnap Phoenix's wife but were unsure who she was. They had mistaken Holly's sister, who fit the profile of a "macaroni and cheese skin" woman, though she seemed too young to be Phoenix's wife. A sudden fright of fear came over Nizzy, and she began to shake. Holly talked to her and reassured her that they couldn't let anyone know they were scared.

Half an hour later, they arrived at the villa. The sisters asked the landlord to show them Phoenix's room, which she did. Inside, they began searching for Phoenix's passport, pants, and shirt. They found that his belongings were all packed away, with gray duct tape wrapped around everything. One suitcase was open, and his bed was neatly made. Holly finally located his passport by tearing the pocket of one of the suitcases.

When the landlord saw Holly retrieve the passport, she went into a frenzy. She called her husband, demanding to know if he was aware that the wife was coming to get it. Her outburst continued as she instructed him to call Annmarie, Phoenix's girlfriend. Suddenly, they were faced with guns pointing at them. Holly felt her extremities getting wet and warm. But she stood her ground, saying, "Shoot me, you idiot. If you kill us, how are you going to claim your money?"

The husband burst into laughter and said, "I'm just kidding," as he rolled on the ground. His wife joined in the laughter, and Holly and Nizzy, though still uneasy, laughed along to diffuse the tension. The landlord then began to pace and reached into her pocket for a pack of cigarettes, asking her husband for a light. She took a deep drag, letting the smoke curl up, almost burning out the cigar, and began speaking again.

"Annmarie and Phoenix had a fight on New Year's Day," she said. "He threw her out at 1 a.m. and told her not to come back. That weekend led to his madness due to some wild, exotic sex. She was so riled up that she climbed the wall to get back in. All the picture frames began to fall. Then he tossed her on the ground."

The landlord was still confused at the fact that the wife had the passport but continued to talk. "The building was vibrating in a series of tremors. She even came out in her underwear, crying for help. She wanted to have a baby with him, but he refused. There was also another girl living on my property with a man from the US. In two years, he married her but that led to his detriment. She robbed him of $65000 and disappeared."

After the lengthy tirade, the sisters told her they had to leave for a doctor's appointment. Holly stepped outside and asked the landlord to move so she could close the door, but she refused. She became very aggressive and blocked her from closing the door.

"Please, madam, can you move so I can close the door?" Holly asked politely.

"Bombo Claught, don't you hear I said you're not going anywhere? We need our money first!" The landlord's aggression made Holly's sister tremble with fear. Holly moved closer, hugged her sister around the waist, and whispered, "Sis, be calm. Don't let them see your fear."

Holly quickly turned to the landlord and reassured her that she would be back if she allowed them to go to the hospital and see the doctor. As they were about to leave, they heard the husband shout, rushing toward them and pressing a gun to their heads while the wife placed hers against Holly's stomach.

"If you ever think about leaving, you'll be dead."

"I know every inch of this area, and you're being watched." Holly was unsure of what to do, but she managed to gather herself, stay calm, and reassure them that they'd be back. Her courage came from one of her brothers, who was a policeman. He once told her that barking dogs seldom bite, and if you're lying, you should say it like you mean it, without any fear. But now she wondered, is he really just barking, or are we actually going to die and disappear without a trace?

At that moment, the wife called Annmarie and told her to meet at the hospital. She sped off, taking the only road out. The sisters followed, but they were quickly left behind in a cloud of dust. Nizzy wanted to leave, but Holly wouldn't let her go. She needed to hear from the doctor about Phoenix's condition. The sisters drove to the hospital, and as they arrived, Holly's sister noticed Phoenix's girlfriend in line.

"Holly, look, isn't that Phoenix's girlfriend?" Holly called her out of the line and said she needed to speak with her.

The wife and the girlfriend stepped away from the crowd to talk privately. Holly could barely speak before the girlfriend burst out, "Phoenix, does he own a big house in the US?"

Holly, confused, replied, "What house?"

The girlfriend continued, "Does he own a Porsche, a Maserati, and a BMW?"

Holly smiled as she sensed the girlfriend's real motives. The girlfriend kept asking question after question, clearly trying to figure out her inheritance if she married Phoenix and he died.

"I heard you have all his money and that you're planning to kill him for it," she accused. Holly felt disgusted by the gold digger and straightened her shoulders, preparing to confront this young woman who still lived with her mother.

"You know what? Yes, we are married, and I control the funds," Holly said in a condescending tone.

The girlfriend looked startled and said, "Phoenix is a liar, and my mom says I should dump him."

In that moment, Holly came up with a plan. "Annmarie, you talk like an idiot because you're young. The man you love is dying - you can't dump him now. Besides, whatever he promised you, I can give it to you. I'm here not to break up your loving relationship but to encourage it," she said, playing along. Two can play this game, Holly thought. The girlfriend quickly rejoined the line, heading off to see her boyfriend. Holly and her sister followed slowly, still gathering information.

When they reached the ward, they were met with chaos. Phoenix, the landlord, and the girlfriend were all shouting at the top of their lungs, arguing about unpaid rent, Phoenix's assets, and other unrelated issues. Holly ignored the commotion and went straight to the nurse's desk to find out what was going on. The nurse informed her that Phoenix had signed himself out again, and they were there to take him home.

Holly quickly said, "No, ma'am, I can't take him - I'm not from here. But I can get his girlfriend to finish the paperwork." Holly walked over to the girlfriend to confirm that she would take Phoenix home.

Suddenly, Phoenix rushed to the nurse's desk and angrily scolded his girlfriend, "Are you that damn young to handle this? You're such a child - try to act like a responsible adult!" Embarrassed, the girlfriend ran off the ward and disappeared once again.

Meanwhile, the landlord, emotionless and insensitive, was still trying to collect rent from Phoenix. As this was happening, Holly leaned over the counter and tried to get more information from the doctor. The doctor and Holly were speaking in low voices and their faces were so close it seemed as if they were about to kiss. Holly whispered to the doctor, "Is it true that Phoenix has a brain hemorrhage?"

"Who told you that?" the doctor asked. Holly pointed to the landlord.

The doctor sighed. "I'm sorry, Holly. Your husband overdosed on LSD, which has caused him to behave erratically and lose his memory. He was also given thallium."

Holly was shocked by this revelation. The doctor explained that they had to administer activated charcoal and other medications to help remove the toxic substances from his system. He then led Holly to a private room to ask her several questions about Phoenix's health while he was living with her, hoping to gain more insight into his condition.

"Has he ever had a seizure?" the doctor asked.

"No," Holly replied. "He only has muscle spasms, but as soon as he takes his medication, he's fine."

The doctor continued to update Holly on Phoenix's condition, sensing that she might have been misled to come to the island. Holly thanked the doctor, smiled, and walked cautiously over to where her sister was standing. She took her sister's hand and said, "Let's go." They began to walk away slowly at first, then faster and faster as they hurried to leave.

Suddenly, Holly felt someone grab her arm.

"Where the hell do you think you're going?"

Holly's sister started trembling with fear again. Holly drew her closer, hugged her, and shrugged the landlord's hand off her arm. The sisters exchanged glances, silently agreeing to say whatever was necessary to convince the landlord they weren't trying to run away.

The landlord had a loud, intimidating voice, so Holly's sister suggested, "Maybe we should go outside or to a restaurant to discuss what you want and how much it will cost."

As they were about to leave, the landlord suddenly asked, "Holly! Do you really want a divorce?"

"Yes, ma'am," Holly answered sharply.

"I have a lawyer who can take care of this right now," the landlord offered.

"Okay, let's go," Holly agreed.

As they were about to exit the hospital, Holly noticed the sky had darkened. The clouds were heavy and low as if a storm was about to break. Seizing the opportunity, the sisters used the weather as an excuse. "Pebbie, it's going to rain. Let's go have lunch instead," Holly suggested to the landlord.

"No," the landlord replied. "What about Phoenix's rent?"

The sisters exchanged looks. "How much do you want?" Holly asked.

"I want this month's rent, plus two months' security deposit and compensation for my distress," the landlord replied straightaway.

The sisters glanced at each other again, realizing they didn't have that kind of money on them. They pretended to consider it and then asked, "How much is his rent?"

For the first time, they were about to discuss actual figures, but the setting was far from ideal. The landlord leaned in close and whispered, "12,000 US dollars per month." She then pulled her phone out of her bag and said, "I need to confirm if Phoenix is really your husband."

Holly was taken aback, giving her a look that said, "Are you serious?" Just as Holly was about to lose her patience, her sister quickly changed the subject to diffuse the tension.

Nizzy blurted out, "Ms. Pebble! She'll get you your money, so let's go to the restaurant and go over the details. Besides, we're hungry."

Pebbie quickly agreed and led them to a nearby restaurant.

The sisters walked in and looked at the menu, but nothing looked appetizing. "We'd rather have Burger King," they suggested.

Pebbie's phone rang, and after a brief conversation, she turned back to the sisters and muttered under her breath, "You damn bitches, I'll see you back at the house. If you even think of leaving, you'll all be dead."

Suddenly, the sisters lost their appetites. They realized they weren't dealing with professionals; these people were just trying to scare them. Holly and her sister left the restaurant and drove to KFC instead. Sitting in the car, they tried to figure out how to escape this situation when, out of frustration, Nizzy shouted, "How dumb can we be? Don't you see our lives are in danger, sis?"

Holly felt torn - part of her wanted to run, but if these people were just bluffing, she knew she had to confront them. For some comfort, Holly suggested they head to Burger King. Once there, she treated them to their favorite meals.

"You're one crazy-ass sis," Nizzy said, shaking her head. "I don't know you. You're bloody suicidal and crazy."

"If I'm going to die, I might as well have my favorite meal first," Holly replied. She ordered a strong cup of coffee and took some Excedrin Migraine tablets, preparing herself for whatever might happen next. Up to that point, they could hardly enjoy their food because of their nerves.

Finally, they gathered the courage to drive to the

landlord's estate. It was a massive twenty-six-bedroom villa, each room with its own bathroom. A huge ballroom with elegant chandeliers overlooked a lush landscape with mini villas and green vegetation.

They were greeted by the sight of Phoenix, sitting hunched over on his bed. The sight terrified Holly, and she wanted to run, but her legs refused to move. She glanced at her sister, who had gone from her usual pale complexion to a bright red, like a bell pepper, trembling with fear.

Holly squeezed her hand and whispered, "Please hold on for a few minutes." She then turned to Pebbie and said, "Could you do us a favor? Nizzy isn't feeling well."

"Holly, take your sister to the car. She's about to pass out," Pebbie said. Taking advantage of the situation, Holly wrapped an arm around Nizzy's waist and guided her to the car, placing her in the driver's seat. As Holly was about to get in, Pebbie grabbed her hair, yanked it back, and demanded to see her marriage certificate. Holly reached into a folder jacket on the back seat, pulled out the certificate, and handed it over. Pebbie released her hair and carefully examined the details in the document.

"I see you are the wife," Pebbie said in a grudgingly respectful tone.

"Yes, ma'am," Holly replied, staring her in the eye to project confidence, although she was afraid.

The landlord echoed her name. "My name is Pebbie."

"Pebbie, my sister is really sick. Can we go now?" Holly asked, using the opportunity to her advantage. Knowing that Nizzy had a severe allergy to peanuts, Holly had told her sister to eat some, hoping the reaction would panic Pebbie enough to let them go.

The plan went off without a hitch. When Pebbie saw Nizzy's face and hands swelling, even Holly acted panicked.

"You effing moron, don't let her die on my property! Take her to the hospital!" Pebbie screamed in alarm.

Holly quickly seized the opportunity. "It's something on the property she's allergic to, and it's highly contagious!" she lied, hoping to intensify Pebbie's panic.

Holly slipped into the passenger seat and whispered urgently to Nizzy, "Drive now and take your meds, fast." They began driving slowly down the steep, winding road as Nizzy angrily swallowed her medication. Holly had never heard her sister use so much profanity before, swearing in every possible way.

Trying not to be harsh, Holly checked the gas gauge and noticed it was full. "Good, no need to stop now," she thought. After driving for a while and covering quite a distance, they finally slowed down to catch their breath. Holly looked at the gas gauge again - it was still at half a tank. That would be more than enough to get them back to Nizzy's house. They continued to drive, and Nizzy continued to curse in utter frustration.

"Let's stop by to see your adoptive sister. Maybe it'll calm you down." Nizzy agreed, knowing the visit might help her relax.

They arrived at her adoptive sister's house and took a walk around, admiring the various herbs she grew for medicinal purposes. Holly couldn't enjoy the educational tour even though the environment was very peaceful. She was paranoid about being followed and was also dealing with Nizzy's anger.

An hour and a half into the tour, Holly's patience ran out. "Can we end this bloody tour already? I need to get home!" she shouted. Her outburst caused her adoptive sister and her family to shift from being excited to looking at her with scorn and disappointment.

Holly quickly realized she had overstepped. She muttered an apology and walked off the property. It was getting late, and Nizzy needed to pick up her son from school, which gave Holly the perfect excuse to leave.

"Nizzy, remember you have to pick up your son," Holly reminded her, hoping it would push them to leave.

"Don't worry," Nizzy called back, "I asked my husband to pick him up, and he's preparing dinner for us."

Under her breath, Holly muttered, "I hate my damn insensitive sister. She thinks she's so great now that she's a doctor." Holly wandered up and down the street before sitting on a rock, murmuring to herself.

Nizzy, meanwhile, was ecstatic, enthusiastically talking

about the different types of herbs and tasting various fruits from the trees. She was critiquing and sharing all the medicinal properties of each herb or fruit she tasted, laughing and smiling joyfully. Everyone else was sharing their thoughts and giggling, clearly enjoying the moment.

Holly wanted to join in the fun but couldn't. She was too consumed with guilt for having put her sister's life in danger and overwhelmed by jealousy, frustration, and a loss of control. Eventually, Nizzy, still somewhat on edge, got into the car, and they drove in silence. Holly apologized, but it fell on deaf ears.

When they arrived at Nizzy's home, she parked the car on the lawn parallel to the garage to leave space for her husband's car. About fifteen minutes later, her husband arrived with the kids. Her two sons jumped out of the car and rushed toward Holly, leaping into her arms and shouting, "Aunty Holly!"

The impact sent Holly crashing to the ground, and everyone laughed loudly - everyone except Nizzy. Holly burst into laughter, hugging and rolling on the ground with the boys, using the moment to shake off her earlier fear. Soon, her nervousness began to fade.

Nizzy called the boys inside to do their homework. Holly watched as they completed their assignments, practiced their piano pieces, and got ready for dinner. The dinner conversation was brief because the kids needed to go to bed early for school the next day. Nizzy tucked them in with bedtime stories and a prayer.

Once the children were fast asleep, Nizzy sat at the table

and, out of nowhere, said to her husband, "My love, I almost died today."

There was a long pause.

"What? And you never called me?" he exclaimed. Another long silence followed. Holly glanced nervously between her sister and her brother-in-law. Knowing he was a soldier in the Army, she braced herself for his reaction.

"My wife!" he shouted, standing up and slamming his fist on the table in a mighty rage.

Nizzy quickly calmed her husband down and started to explain what had happened and why she couldn't call him at that moment. They lost track of time as they sat at the table discussing their next steps. Holly was exhausted, so Nizzy offered her some vodka mixed with orange juice. Holly drank it in one gulp, which made everyone laugh. "Holly, you should sip it," they said.

At that moment, Holly reached an emotional breaking point. She asked for a few more drinks, which they gave her, and soon she began to giggle. She sat down at the piano and started playing, forgetting the children were already fast asleep. Holly played and played until her fingers hurt and tears streamed down her cheeks. Finally, she lay down on the couch, trying to hold back her tears, but they continued to flow until she eventually cried herself to sleep.

The next day, when Nizzy tried to start the car to go to work, she realized it wouldn't start - the tank was empty. "We came home on an empty tank," she marveled. The sisters looked at each other and burst out laughing. The love and bond they shared made it easy to forgive each other. Holly decided to take a breath of fresh air and went for a walk, believing everything would be alright.

She walked until she saw a Rastaman selling coconuts. His locks were neatly bundled, and his beard, twisted into two, reached down to his waist. He wore leather sandals, black fitted pants, and a sleeveless shirt that showed off his rugged muscles. Holly approached him and asked for a coconut. He chopped it briskly and then added a splash of rum. Holly then sat on a rock, falling into a trance as she listened to his music. A song played in the background. Holly bought another coconut and then excused herself.

As she walked away, the Rastaman called out, "Walk good and take care of yourself; you're too pretty to look so calamitous."

Holly paused, confused. "Cala who?"

"Lady, I don't know your name, but you're too gorgeous to look so disheartened," he clarified as his hidden smile became evident in his voice. A small smile played on Holly's lips, and she took the compliment to heart. She started to speak confidence over herself, thinking, *I have to pull myself together.*

The next day, Nizzy took Holly to the airport and bid her goodbye.

A year later, Holly's husband called to say he had decided to stay in the land of paradise with his girlfriend. Her heart shattered all over again. She had been clinging to a broken love and unrealistic expectations. The pain deepened, and she became aloof. She grew to hate all men, walking around with a fake smile, pretending to be happy. She moved through life like a shadow, a ticking time bomb, pretending to have it all together.

Holly had given up on life yet acted like everything was fine. Many guys asked her out, but she found excuses to say no. Holly dug a hole and stayed in it; it became her way of life.

Chapter 2: The Taboo Lilly

Three years had gone by.

Now, after so many years, she received a message from an old friend. They had been best friends since high school and, at one point, were even high school sweethearts. Over the years, they had kept in touch, but their friendship had always remained just that - friendship. Holly was afraid to date him, fearing that losing their friendship would tear her apart. They spoke on the phone for hours, recalling about their past and catching up on their present lives. They talked about anything and everything. It was evident they enjoyed each other's company.

One day, he called her and asked if she would like to meet him for old time's sake. Without hesitation, Holly agreed. She didn't stop to think about what it might mean or how it might feel; all she knew was that she was going to meet her best friend. Excited and happy about the prospect, she took a quick shower and began getting ready.

But as she got dressed, she suddenly felt nervous. Her heart started pounding in her chest, and she felt like she couldn't breathe. Butterflies filled her stomach as she slipped into a backless red pencil dress. Holly curled her hair and looked at herself in the mirror. She applied a bold red lipstick, but suddenly, panic took over. Out of nowhere, she began to undress and broke down in tears.

She cried for an hour, overawed by the fear of taking this

step. Holly realized she had grown comfortable in her cocoon of isolation, and stepping out of it now felt terrifying. She was running late but managed to pull herself together. Ultimately, she decided to go for a semi-casual outfit instead. She couldn't face him looking so sexy. Various thoughts raced through her mind. *What if he thinks I'm hitting on him? What if I come on too strong?*

Holly chose something more comfortable, ran out of the house, got in her car, and set the GPS. As she drove, her thoughts ran wild, and a headache started to form. She turned on the radio, hoping for something soothing, but quickly changed the stations one after another. She knew there could be no sexual contact between them - he was just a friend. Yet, her naive thoughts made her panic. Driving became difficult as her emotions spiraled out of control.

When she arrived at the hotel, she waited in the lobby, still feeling very nervous. As soon as he saw her, he hastened his steps, grabbed her, and kissed her passionately. Holly's knees grew weak, and she quickly pulled away, bracing herself against the wall to catch her breath. *What the hell am I getting myself into?* she thought. *How can this be love? I can't even love myself, much less another. Is this love?*

He gently wrapped his arm around her waist, pulled her closer, and whispered, "Let's go." There was a gentle smile on his face. Holly followed, feeling both lost and exhilarated, as he kissed her on the forehead. She felt out of place, torn between the fantasy of a romantic movie and the reality of her life. *Is this love or just the desire to feel wanted?* She wondered.

They took the elevator to the fifth floor, and when they walked into the room, Holly's excitement grew. The room looked perfect, like something out of a magazine. At first, she hesitated. *This can't be real,* she thought. He took her bag and placed it on the sofa, but Holly remained frozen, yearning for something to snap her back to reality.

Then she felt his warm hands holding hers, gently pulling her closer. Holly was speechless. He moved his fingers gently across her face, then teasingly across her lips. Holly's heart started to race; she knew she couldn't make love to him, but he had no idea. He moved closer again and whispered, "Let's go out and eat."

Holly stuttered, managing to ask, "Where?"

He smiled and replied, "Do you have somewhere in mind?"

"Ah… I'm fine, thank you," Holly replied nervously.

He sensed the nervousness and held her hand gently. He then looked into her eyes, smiled, and said, "Holly, I'm taking you somewhere to eat. Is that okay for you?"

Holly nodded her head and picked up her coat hanging in the closet. As they stepped outside the hotel, the chauffeur opened the car door for her, and she slid into the back seat. Her companion thanked the chauffeur with a joyful tone before the car smoothly pulled away from the curb. He looked at her blushed face and smiled. As they drove along the highway, he reached out and placed his hand gently over hers. Holly smiled, and they locked eyes, both savoring the moment. He looked at her again and said with a warm smile, "We're almost there."

He took her to a five-star restaurant overlooking the ocean. They were escorted to their table, which was elegantly set for two with candlelight. He pulled out her chair for her, then sat down himself. Reaching across the table, he held her hands and drew her closer. Holly stood up, and they shared a kiss across the table.

As Holly glanced around, she searched for any sign of champagne or wine, but the absence didn't bother her. She remembered how he would get tipsy just from the smell of alcohol, which she used to justify her thoughts. She noticed that he didn't eat much from his plate while Holly finished everything on hers. She felt his eyes lingering on her, and to distract herself, she made silly jokes. He chuckled and continued to gaze at her, saying, "You are so radiantly beautiful; you are like a garden of white lilies, unblemished."

He held her hands and gently wiped her slender fingers. Holly knew she needed to feel comfortable and let go of her past. *This is your moment,* she thought. *Let your hair down and live it as if it will never come again.*

As they prepared to leave, he wrapped his arm around her waist and kissed her cheek. They walked together toward the ocean and left their shoes behind on the white sand. They laughed, chased each other, and finally sat down on a bench to watch the sunset. "Let's get back to the hotel," Zahir whispered in her ear.

When they returned to the hotel, Holly sank into the sofa as she was exhausted from the long day. She closed her eyes for a few moments. Zahir went to the bathroom, and she assumed he was going to take a shower. He soon came back and sat beside her. They began to kiss, and before long, their clothes were scattered across the room.

Zahir held her hands and asked what kind of music she liked. He walked over to his laptop and played some soft, slow jams. He reached out, drew her close, and they danced sensually together. He led her to the bathroom, where candlelight was softly glowing around the Jacuzzi, and a bottle of champagne was placed in a wine holder, wrapped in a white towel. Holly thought this might be part of the hotel's special amenities. She was swept off her feet.

Although the setting was romantic, Holly felt a twinge of regret. She knew she couldn't make love to her best friend, which made her heartache even more. She hesitated, trying to prolong the moment. Finally, with a heavy heart, she whispered her circumstances into his ear. He responded simply, "I know."

Romantic killer am I, she thought. Holly lay upon his chest through the night; she knew he was very disappointed yet so supportive.

Soon enough, sunlight made its way into the room. Holly and Zahir went to the lounge for breakfast, then returned to their room to dine. Zahir spread butter on her toast and playfully held it up to her mouth. Just as she was about to take a bite, he pulled it away and laughed. He fed her teasingly, then added sugar to her tea and tasted it to ensure it was perfect. They laughed and chatted and enjoyed each other's company.

Holly asked if he would bathe with her. He eagerly agreed, turned on the taps, and added cherry blossom bubble soap to the water. As the bubbles began to form, he started to kiss her. They quickly shed their clothes and settled into the bath. Zahir pulled her close, massaging her back, then her neck and his hands began to wander lower. Holly turned to reciprocate. Soon, their movements became synchronized.

He stood up, stepped out of the bath, and grabbed a towel. Leading her to the bedroom, he gently lifted her off the ground and slowly lowered her onto his shaft. Holly began to tremble, having not been intimately touched for the past three years. He laid her down began to showoff his foreplay skills. Then, he whispered, "I'll be gentle, just relax." Slowly, he entered her, and they made love. Soon, they both climaxed and collapsed against each other, breathless and holding hands.

Time passed quickly, and it was soon time for him to return to work, which meant another six-hour drive. Holly's aloof side emerged. "So, you used me for sex, and now you're leaving?"

He turned around and gave her a hug. "I searched for you all these years. Now that I've found you, I wanted to show you how much I care." Just then, his phone rang. "Sorry, love, I have to take this call." The conversation went on for several minutes, during which he spoke in French. "Let's make this deal work; I'll see you in a few."

Holly thanked him and apologized for her rudeness, feeling like a romantic killer. He was very understanding, kissed her to reassure her, and expressed that he had a wonderful time and looked forward to seeing her again.

They left the hotel in separate cars. As Holly drove home, she couldn't grasp what had just happened. It felt like she was living in a fantasy movie.

She dialed his number, and he answered on the first ring.

"Hello?" he answered joyfully.

"Hi, hi, and hi," she found herself repeating.

"Oh, hi, dear."

"Oh dear, please forgive me," Holly replied.

"For what?" he responded in a sensual tone.

Unable to find a clear explanation, she blurted out, "Do you love me? Please, just let me know." The real question she faced was whether she wanted to be loved or merely played with.

He chuckled softly, then paused. The anticipation was getting the best of her.

"Holly, I love you with all my heart. You are very special to me, and I had one of the most wonderful times with you this weekend. You make me very happy, and I hope to see you very soon."

Holly knew he had a demanding schedule, always in and out of meetings or busy showing houses to clients. "Thank you. That means the world to me," she said.

"I have to go now, but before you hang up, turn your radio to 97.1. That song is for you, from me," he replied.

Holly ended the call, turned on her GPS, and switched to the radio. As the song played, Holly began to bawl. Tears streamed down her cheeks and onto her lap. She tried to convince herself that she wasn't in love and that this was just a fleeting moment. When she reached her destination, she crawled into bed, hugged her pillows, and fell asleep, feeling an unexpected happiness.

As she drifted off in sleep, she thought, *a girl is allowed to dream, to fall into fantasy, to hop around in fairyland, but reality and responsibilities soon knock at the door. Life can change in an instant.*

Chapter 3: The Pitfall

Holly had fallen many times, feeling stuck in a constant cycle of fear and sadness. As she got older, she started to see the pattern of her struggles. But every time, she found strength inside herself and realized she had always moved from bleakness to self-growth.

Months after experiencing a brief moment of happiness, she fell into another pit. Living paycheck to paycheck with two children in university, she faced extreme hardship. It was a period of dirt-poor living. Holly lived in continuous fear of losing the fragile stability holding her family together. And then, that dreaded day arrived - she lost her job.

Holly was forced to give up her apartment. Her funds quickly dwindled. The basics - food, shelter, clothing - were gone. Each morning, she prayed, searched for jobs, and struggled to complete her degree assignments. A thick fog of homelessness loomed over her. She realized she was no different from any other homeless person who had been through this and survived. Depression became her adversary, and she began to reflect on her past, wondering how she had reached this point.

Marrying at a young age had seemed like a good idea, even though the marriage had been abusive. Her ex-husband turned out to be a pedophile. Once Holly no longer resembled a young girl, he started cheating with his students. Night after night, he would taunt her, saying, "When are you leaving, bitch? Can't you see you're expired?"

Very soon, Holly was kicked out of the house she had bought with her husband, along with their two children. At that time, the older child was in high school, and the younger one was just four years old. Her best friend Jordon helped her find a two-bedroom house, but the only thing in it was a sink. With some credit, she bought two beds, a stove, and a refrigerator. Work, night classes, and books became her best friends as she juggled everything - helping her kids with their homework and taking them to activities.

There were many nights when Holly cried endlessly. She had no help from her family or from the children's father. But she persevered and eventually earned her bachelor's degree. It was a happy moment for her - she graduated at the top of her class with honors and distinction. Just two months before her graduation, she traveled to the United States to complete her registration at Howard University. She felt her life was taking a positive turn. She received a full scholarship and a paid teaching job.

However, when Holly returned to her home country, she faced more abuse from her husband. "You moron, you think you're better than me," he would shout, full of jealousy. He wouldn't let her see anyone, even though he didn't want to be with her. One day, before Holly could even speak, he punched her hard, knocking her to the ground. Her children ran out crying, trying to help their mother, but he pushed them aside. Holly tried to crawl away, but he grabbed her hair, kicked her in the stomach, and punched her in the face again and again.

She thought it was over, but it wasn't. She cried for help, but no one came. Suddenly, he broke a bottle and came at her again. Holly raised her hand to protect her face, and the bottle slashed her hand.

Blood poured everywhere.

That attack sent her to the hospital. Holly almost lost her life that day. Her husband had wanted to scar her emotionally and destroy her beauty. She lost the tendons in her right hand, but after surgery, she learned to use both hands. Despite all of this, she still attended her graduation.

Holly thought the abuse would end after everything he had done to her, but she was wrong. He only escalated his attacks. Weeks later, he got her fired from her job and took her to court, trying to have her arrested. He even sued her for child support, which she thought was ridiculous. The legal battles didn't stop. He sued her again when she tried to see her children. Holly was constantly in and out of court, fighting every case. She couldn't even go to the mall without being followed - not by the police, but by her husband.

Holly once read, "If you must leave a place that you have lived in and loved, and where all your yesteryears are buried deep, leave it, and if your life is threatened, leave it the fastest way you can. Never turn back and never believe that an hour you remember is a better hour because it is dead."

Chapter 4: The Change

Holly's life was now in danger, so she fled, seeking refuge. It was incredibly difficult, especially leaving her home to move to a continent where she knew no one except her aunt, who hosted her for some time. Holly worked for her as she pursued her doctorate. Life changed when she was finally able to bring her kids to join her. But soon after, they were forced out of the house without notice. Holly couldn't comprehend where life was taking her.

Holly was worried. Yet, she shook off the weight of despair and was determined to move forward. 'Life goes on. I'm not dead,' she reminded herself.

She found a small apartment where they could all stay while she worked to stabilize their lives. One day, she found a discarded piece of furniture that turned out to be a hidden treasure. Unfortunately, the apartment was infested with bedbugs, a problem she was unaware of when she brought the furniture inside. For four weeks, they endured the discomfort and stress of the infestation. Holly contacted the apartment management, who sent maintenance to investigate.

When the maintenance worker discovered the bedbugs, Holly asked, "What are bedbugs, and how did we get them?" Her voice was polite but tinged with frustration. The maintenance worker looked at them as if they were from another planet. Sympathetic to their situation, he explained the causes of the infestation and provided advice on how to eliminate the pests. Now armed with knowledge, Holly and her family were determined to overcome this latest challenge.

Later, Holly was promoted and began earning more. She spoke with the dean and put her education on hold as her two daughters excelled in school. Ten years later, Holly lost her job. Her second daughter had just finished her first year at an Ivy League college, while the eldest was pursuing a master's at a prestigious School of Architecture in California. Nonetheless, life continued to throw curveballs. The harder Holly tried, the more things seemed to fall apart. She couldn't understand it. Life felt like a wheel - she never knew what was around the corner. She experienced periods of success, happiness, and prosperity, only to be followed by challenges, setbacks, and difficulties. Sometimes, she was up; other times, she had nothing.

Holly moved from living happily to surviving from paycheck to paycheck, eventually facing homelessness. Fear continued to gnaw at her soul. She cried, drowning herself in tears and self-pity – it was the most fluent language she had learned. Communication broke down in her home. She thought about the many struggles - sleeping, fatigue, boredom, killing time, storage, health, harassment, and countless other unpredictable difficulties - everyday 'murders' that wore her down. But fighting back became her greatest tool for survival.

She drove to the library to complete an online exam and fill out job applications. Despite the darkness, she clung to hope - hope is being able to see a light at the end of the tunnel.

But when she arrived at the library, she found that her laptop had stopped working. Reaching for her phone, she realized her service had been cut off for non-payment. Holly put her hand over her mouth and groaned. Her lungs seized with pain, and her heart seemed to cave in. Tears fell in clumps, soaking her silk shirt and exposing her trembling body.

"How can this be?" Holly asked herself. Just then, the librarian approached and gently asked if she needed help. Taking a deep breath, Holly calmed herself. He led her to a private room where she could use a desktop computer. Somehow, she managed to barely pass the exam. That day, she felt the full weight of a midlife crisis.

"What the hell *is* a midlife crisis?" she muttered to herself.

She knew she was too young for it, yet she felt every ounce of it. Her thoughts drifted back to her younger days when her principal, who was also her boss at the time, used to tell her,

"Obstacles are what you see when you take your eyes off your goals."

Goal! The word echoed in her mind.

"I've lost my goal," Holly whispered, repeating it to herself over and over.

Feeling defeated, she headed home and collapsed into bed, trying to find a sense of purpose. She remembered she still needed a phone, so she called in a favor. As soon as the phone was charged, she lay down, only to be startled by a strange sound.

Croak, croak, croak.

Holly jumped up. Her heart was racing. "Oh my…," she gasped. "Is there a frog in my room?"

Then she remembered - it was her new ringtone. She exhaled and answered the call. It was Pebbie, her landlord, on the other end.

"Holly!" Pebbie's voice was shaky and full of anxiety.

Holly sighed, already bracing herself. "What's wrong now, Ms. Pebbie?"

"Phoenix tried to kill me! There's a warrant out for his arrest."

"What?" Holly sat up straighter. "What happened?"

Without waiting for a response, Pebbie launched into the story. "After his girlfriend dumped him, Phoenix lost it. I went over to break up a fight, and he pulled a sword on me! He swung it at my chest, and I barely stepped back in time. I fell and screamed for help. People in the neighborhood came running, and Phoenix fled. We can't find him. Holly, I hope you're not hosting a criminal."

The conversation dragged on for nearly an hour as Pebbie unloaded her fears. Finally, she paused. "Holly, are you still there?"

"Yes, ma'am," Holly replied. "I'm just listening. I'm glad you're okay. Can I call you back? My phone's about to die."

After hanging up, Holly lay back down, but sleep evaded

her. Frustrated, she got up for a drink, only to hear her phone ring again. This time, it was Phoenix.

"What does he want now? Oh no, don't tell me he's at my door!" Holly was talking to herself. She steadied her breath and tried to calm the panic that froze her in place. She glanced at her phone, then drank some water before collapsing back onto the bed.

The next day, her daughter had planned a book review with some friends. Once all the guests arrived, they read for a while before launching into a heated discussion. The room buzzed with intensity as they debated, each one trying to make their point agree yet disagree. Holly decided to get up and offer everyone some drinks. As she moved slowly toward the kitchen, she noticed someone strange lounging on the large bean bag in the corner, looking half-drunk.

Holly frowned.

That couldn't be… there was no alcohol served.

She walked over and asked, "Excuse me, sir, are you okay?"

To her horror, it was Phoenix. Her heart pounded and cold sweat dripped down her face as she stood there, stunned.

"Holly, don't just stand there; get the juice!" one of her daughter's friends called out, unaware of what was happening. But Holly couldn't move. She was paralyzed. Her mind was racing as she tried to process what was going on. She wanted to scream, but no sound came out.

Just then, a tall, dark, handsome man stepped forward and caught her as she began to collapse. It was Zahir. His light brown eyes sparkled, and his nicely toned muscles and perfect smile, complete with dimples, captivated everyone's attention. He had just arrived in town and heard from a friend about the gathering Holly's daughter was hosting. Wanting to surprise her, he invited himself.

Now a successful millionaire with multiple businesses, Zahir took charge as panic spread through the room. He gently tried to make Holly conscious, jokingly waving someone's cheesy shoe over her nose as her daughters fanned her and called her name, frantic for her to wake up.

Paula grabbed a glass of water and splashed it in Holly's face.

Suddenly, Holly shot up and yelled.

"What is going on?" Holly gasped, disoriented, as she looked around. Everyone started clapping and cheering, thinking it was all an act. But Holly was confused and flustered as she found herself in Zahir's arms. Overwhelmed, she fainted again.

This time, Zahir gently kissed her lips. As he moved her away slowly, Holly's eyes fluttered open. He kissed her again, and before long, they were lost in each other, forgetting the guests around them. Realizing what was happening, Holly's daughter, embarrassed, shouted, "Mom!"

Holly quickly snapped out of it and composed herself.

"I'm so sorry," she apologized to her daughter and the guests. Embarrassed, she hurried to the bedroom to change and convinced herself that it had all been some strange dream.

As soon as she took off her clothes, the closet door suddenly popped open. Before she could react, Phoenix grabbed her from behind and clamped a hand over her mouth. Holly's heart raced. In the heat of passion, Zahir had followed her to check on her. He knocked on the bedroom door but got no answer. Sensing something was wrong, he tried to break the door down but failed.

Chaos erupted. The party was over, and within seconds, everyone had rushed out. The staircase echoed with footsteps like the rumbling of an earthquake. Women were screaming, and men were leaping down several steps at a time, desperate to reach safety. Residents flung their doors open, trying to see what was causing the chaos. Phoenix, still holding Holly hostage, pulled out a gun and demanded space to leave. Holly's two daughters screamed in terror as they watched Phoenix drag her through the door and down the stairs. A shot was heard, and all the nosey people shut their doors in fear for their lives.

Holly couldn't make a sound, but she had a plan. She prayed it would work, especially since she was in so much danger. Phoenix turned to Zahir and shouted, "Are you the one screwing this bitch? Stay the hell away, or I'll kill you both!"

Holly's stomach churned in pain, and her voice grew hoarse from screaming. With no other options, she bit down hard on Phoenix's hand, tore apart a piece of flesh, and spat it to the ground. Blood spurted from his veins like a burst pipe. He let go of her and clutched his injured hand. In that split second, Holly rushed toward Zahir.

Phoenix was now losing a lot of blood. He staggered to his car, firing stray bullets into the air as he tried to escape. Neighbors called the police. The flashing lights and sirens filled the streets as officers chased after Phoenix, calling for backup. His car came to a stop, and the police shouted, "Come out with your hands in the air!" They repeated the command over and over, but there was no response. As they approached and opened the car door, Phoenix fell out onto the ground. They handcuffed him and took him to the hospital, where he was placed under suicide watch.

When Phoenix regained consciousness and realized he was still alive, he let out a furious roar. They had to restrain him and give him a sedative to calm him down. Eventually, Phoenix was transferred to a psychiatric ward for treatment. A year later, he died from a drug overdose, which ultimately led to his death.

Holly was in shock over what had just happened. Her two children hugged and kissed her while Zahir took her and the kids to a safe place. Although Holly was relieved by this new chapter in her life, nightmares haunted her. She started to lose hope. First, she told herself she was too old to be loved by anyone. She often stood in front of the mirror and searched for validation. She compared her life to her six brothers and seven sisters, who were all well-established, and then broke down in tears. Holly began questioning everything in her life. Her daughters could often hear her crying out, "What have I done to deserve this?"

As time passed, Holly's children grew worried as she refused to leave her room. She lay in bed, weeping endlessly, as the darkness of depression consumed her. The strain took a toll on her daughters, who were both preparing to return to college. The eldest was heading to San Diego to finish her master's in architecture, while the younger one was in her second year. They needed a miracle.

Zahir, who lived in a penthouse in New York City, was a wealthy but reserved man. Although he was very rich, he didn't enjoy partying or drinking. He spent his time reading, playing golf, donating to charity, and giving motivational speeches. His busy schedule made it difficult for Holly's children to reach him.

A miracle seemed impossible, but sometimes, the greatest miracles come when we least expect them.

Chapter 5: Lost and Alone

One day, the sisters decided to drive to New York with the hope that Zahir could help their mother. When they arrived, they found it wasn't easy to get past security. The guards at the door refused to let them in. Fortunately, it was a hot summer day. Paula, the elder daughter, came up with a plan. She went to a store and bought some eye-catching dresses. She told her younger sister to find a single man going into the building. When her sister spotted one, she approached him and held his hand as if they were together. It was a risky move, but they had to try to see Zahir.

Once her sister got inside, Paula created a distraction for the security guards, which allowed her sister to rush to Zahir's office. Zahir was surprised to see her, not knowing who she was at first. Samantha, the younger sister, shouted, "Zahir, it's me, Samantha - Holly's daughter! It's me!!!"

There was a brief silence as Zahir reached out and hugged her. Just as he was about to ask why she was there, Paula yelled, "Samantha, help me!"

At that moment, Paula was seized by the security guards. Zahir rushed outside and instructed the guards to bring her to him. He began laughing hysterically while the girls exchanged uneasy glances, realizing they hadn't achieved their goal and found the situation far from amusing.

"Do you want something to eat or drink?" Zahir asked, but the girls shook their heads.

"Why are you here?" he inquired.

"My mom!" Samantha said before Zahir could speak further.

Zahir began to rave about Holly, saying, "Oh, she is such a beauty, a lady of class." Then he fell silent, lost in thoughts of how pleasurable it would be to have her in bed. Despite his attempts over the years, she had always turned him down, except for one moment.

"Mr. Zahir," the girls whispered, trying to get his attention.

"My mom needs you!" Samantha yelled.

"Needs me? What happened to her?" Zahir asked in a worried voice. He was now fully attentive.

Samantha shouted, "Mom is dying!"

Zahir lightly tapped Samantha on the shoulder and said, "Young ladies, if your mom is that serious, why are we standing here?"

He was eager to rush to their mother's aid but also wanted to make sure he wasn't being tricked by two young women. He studied their faces, looking for any sign of deceit, but they gave him their most sincere expressions. Zahir was taken in by their earnestness. He gave them some money and offered to let them stay the night and leave for home the next day. The girls declined and insisted they needed to get back immediately to be with their mother.

As they were about to leave, Zahir asked, "Does your mom know you're here?" He looked at them with suspicion.

"Oh no, sir," they replied and walked away.

Samantha was disgusted by Zahir's arrogance. She turned back and said, "By the way, I can see why Mom didn't choose you. You pretend to be nice, but deep down, you're just like the others - snobby and rich, thinking you're better than everyone else. I hope Mom never speaks to you again. Mean old man!"

Samantha sobbed as her sister comforted her. "Come on, sis, let's go home."

Zahir watched them leave and instructed one of his security guards to follow them. Soon after, the girls were back home, anxiously hoping their mother was okay. They opened the door slowly and were surprised to find their mom standing there.

"Where have you been?" she yelled. "I thought something happened to you both." She hugged them and invited them to join her for dinner. The girls were puzzled about what had transpired between their trip to New York and their return home.

"Well, girls," their mom said. "I know I've been depressed lately, but while you were away, I decided to make a change in my life. I'm not dead yet, so why should I act like I am? I'm going to put on my best clothes and go out tonight to have some fun."

The girls exchanged looks and then chuckled. They were somewhat relieved.

"Okay, Mom!" they said in unison.

They had dinner together and shared some jokes. Then, Samantha excused herself from the table to get ready for an event before heading off to college. She planned to visit a church. When she was about to enter the bathroom to shower, a knock on the door interrupted her. The girls exchanged confused glances. Paula went to answer the door and was surprised to find Zahir standing there. She called for Samantha, who rushed from the bathroom. The sisters quickly ushered Zahir back and asked, "What are you doing here?"

"Girls, I'm here to see your mom. Could you please let her know?" Zahir asked.

They went back inside to find their mother ready.

"Oh, Mom, you look pretty today," the girls said, trying to distract her. Holly sensed something was off due to their behavior.

"What now, girls? What do you want?" Holly asked.

"Oh, Mom, you're so gorgeous," Samantha said.

"Mom, why don't we walk you to the door?" Paula suggested.

Holly thought they were being silly but picked up her purse and car keys. The girls giggled as they guided her toward the door. When Holly opened it, she was surprised to see Zahir holding a bouquet of roses. Overjoyed, she jumped into his arms without taking the flowers. Zahir nearly lost his balance but managed to hold her up, twirling her around before gently setting her down. They hugged and shared a kiss. The girls laughed and closed the door behind them. They were very happy to see their mom so joyful.

Holly tried to pull away, but Zahir gently caught her hand and pulled her back into his arms. The girls were overjoyed to see their mother so happy. Holly knew this moment was fleeting, so she canceled her plans for the evening. It was too late to prepare a meal for her unexpected guest. As she turned to leave, Zahir gently grabbed her arms, and Holly found herself pressed against his chest. He used his long, slender fingers to tease her lips, causing her knees to buckle. As she stumbled, Zahir caught her and tilted her back, gazing into her eyes before gently setting her upright. Holly's emotions were overwhelming. She couldn't catch her breath, so she retreated to her room and closed the door behind her. She pressed her fingers to her lips, trying to process the whirlwind of emotions she was feeling. Zahir chuckled, knocked on the door, and asked if she was okay. Holly broke down in tears, realizing that this moment of happiness for her was short-lived. She felt like a child playing in a dollhouse, unaware of the hidden dangers. She sensed that Zahir had been keeping secrets from her all these years.

Finally, Zahir confessed, "Holly, I'm married. I have to go back to my wife and children." A wave of anger washed over Holly.

The lies…

The deceit…

The realization that she was just a pawn in his game…

How could he love someone else and share his dreams with her?

Holly struggled with the social norms her mother had always instilled in her: never sleep with a married man. Her religious beliefs flashed through her mind. She had married as a faithful wife, only to be abandoned to raise two children alone. After thirteen years of marriage, her first husband had left her for a younger woman and deemed her 'expired.' She was ruined, with no job or house but breath in her body. She fought the odds, ran to another country, and started all over. Her second had vanished to an island with a teenager. Now, here she was, entangled with another married man who was using her to fill a void. He was now going back to his wife and children.

Holly turned and slapped Zahir very hard. Then, she shouted and demanded, "What the hell are you doing here? Get out of my house, go back to your wife, you cheating jerk! Can't you have a shred of loyalty?" She pleaded with him to leave.

Holly stayed in bed for weeks and locked herself away from the world. Her children couldn't coax her out, but they had important news to share.

"Mom? Mother? Mummy?" Samantha called out as she knocked on Holly's bedroom door. "My sister and I need to talk to you.”

Holly was exhausted and emotionally drained, but she didn't want to disappoint her daughters again. She pulled herself together and promised she would join them for breakfast.

The family sat in silence as the girls tried to find the right way to break the news. Finally, Paula cleared her throat.

“Mom,” she began hesitantly. “I don’t know how you’ll feel about this, but... Dad is coming to visit us.”

The room fell dead silent. Holly’s heart raced as she tried to grasp what she had just heard.

“WHAT?!” she exclaimed in a voice raised in shock. She forced a strained smile and stood up from the table. After a moment, she calmed herself and asked, “And when exactly is he coming? Where is he planning to stay?”

After a long, tense conversation, Holly learned that her ex-husband would be staying nearby - too close for comfort, right by her apartment. She shook her head as she tried to process the news. How could she say no after eleven years of them not seeing him?

“Okay,” she finally said.

That night, Holly cried harder than she had in a long time. She was already struggling financially, barely able to pay rent, and hoping for a miracle. Now this. She had been applying for jobs, but nothing had come through. Driving for Uber was the only source of income keeping her afloat, and even that wasn't enough. Despite everything, Holly hoped for something positive to come out of the situation.

The girls filled her in on their father's life. Holly learned he had remarried and had more children. Time moved slowly for Holly as she watched Samantha practicing her K-pop dance routine during the day, hoping to win a contest and earn some money. Later that night, Paula came home late, and Holly asked why.

"Mom," Paula sighed. "Daddy's coming in two weeks, and I need to book a hotel for him. I don't want him staying here."

Holly was exhausted from everything happening around her. It felt like the harder she tried to make her life a bit easier, the more it got worse.

Finally, Holly said to Paula, "I'll provide meals for the length of time he'll be here."

Holly knew that her bank account was dwindling, and she was just living off the little she had stored away from driving Uber.

'Everything will be fine…' Holly whispered to herself.

That night, she went down on her knees and cried out again while the girls were playing games and catching up on each other's lives.

"God, the food is running low, the roof over our heads could be gone any day, our clothes are worn and tattered, and some of our shoes have holes. I pray for a way out of this."

The next morning, she awoke to sunlight streaming through the window directly onto her face. Rubbing her eyes, she pinched herself to make sure she was still alive. Zahir was gone, and her pride wouldn't let her reach out to him for help. Holly couldn't bear to hurt another family. Her marriage had been destroyed by a teenage girl, and she had seen too many marriages fall apart because of similar circumstances, though some had weathered the storm.

It was now Saturday, just two days before her rent was due. Holly picked up her checkbook and paid the next month's rent, knowing that if nothing changed soon, she would have to file for bankruptcy. She prayed, cried, and then began her job search again. She found the last $20 in her purse and looked over her jewelry, considering what she could pawn just to buy food. The car payments were overdue, and she feared the car would be repossessed soon.

Standing on the balcony, Holly watched the world go by - birds flying, children laughing and playing, tenants arguing. She chuckled and whispered under her breath, "Why is my life so hard?"

She packed her bag and was about to quietly leave the apartment, careful not to disturb her sleeping daughters or her ex, who was now in another room. Tears ran down her face, and she whispered to herself that all hope was gone unless a miracle happened.

Holly let out a bittersweet chuckle and, with a wry smile,

cried out, "My first husband was a priest, and he left me for a fifteen-year-old girl… Annmarie. The second left me too…" She laughed at the irony and shook her head as she knelt down again, pouring her heart out. Her knees grew sore under the weight of her petite body, so she shifted to sit and continued her prayer.

Suddenly, there was a knock. The door to her room creaked open slightly. Holly turned as her heart pounded… no one else was in the house. "How can this be?" she whispered. The door opened further, and a bright beam of light flooded the room. Holly's breath was caught in her throat; she thought she had seen a ghost.

She stood frozen in place. She was dumbstruck.

Who could she possibly tell about this without being dismissed as crazy?

She rubbed her eyes, unsure if it had all been a dream. Eventually, she decided to visit her aunt, who had called earlier in the week about going shopping for her grandson's birthday. Holly drove some Uber rides afterward to make ends meet.

Later that day, after a short nap, she woke up to find that her bank account had been wiped clean.

"How can this be?" she screamed.

Holly broke down in tears and canceled all her appointments for the day. Her body was too weak to carry on. "How will I pay the rent, the car note, the light bill, buy food…?" she muttered as the overwhelming list of expenses ran through her mind. The money in her account was nearly gone. She paced the apartment while crying. Despair filled her heart, and for the first time, she seriously considered ending her life. Dark thoughts swirled in her mind, but she fought them off.

Clutching her stomach, Holly cried until she collapsed to the floor, curling into a tight ball to comfort herself. Her nails dug into her skin as she squeezed her body, but the emotional pain was so great she barely felt the physical hurt. She stretched out flat on the floor and pounded her fists against the ground until she noticed blood seeping from her wounds. Unfazed, she got up, dressed the cuts, and called the rental office, hoping to request an extension, only to find they had already processed the check.

Holly was now determined not to give up. She dressed and went to the bank, hoping... for a miracle, perhaps. She drove for Uber every day, without a single break, desperate to make ends meet. Somehow, she kept going. Her rent was paid, and there was food on the table for her and her two children.

On the morning of July 6th, Holly sat with her Bible and stared at the list of goals she had tucked inside. Tears ran down her face as she gazed at it for hours.

Just then, her phone rang. She answered it and was greeted with, "Holly, we have a health insurance plan for you."

Holly chuckled softly and replied, "I already have insurance." She hung up and felt a new hope in her heart as if a door was being opened for her.

Holly had applied for a job that required her to take a test on Sunday. She got up early, completed the test, and was thrilled to learn she had passed. After that, she prepared for church. Climbing the three flights of stairs to her apartment left her breathless, and by the time she reached the door, she was exhausted. She quietly opened it, not wanting to disturb her daughters, who were laughing and chatting over breakfast. Slipping past them, she headed straight to her room.

The noise from the closet alerted the girls that she was home, and they came in for a brief chat before hurrying to get ready - they were already running late. Within ten minutes, the three of them were heading out.

While descending the stairs, disaster struck. On the third step, Holly's heel got stuck, sending her tumbling forward. She reached out for the railing, but it was too late.

Buff!

She hit the floor, then rolled down several steps before landing face-first at the bottom. Her daughters screamed in panic.

"Mom, are you okay?" they asked in voices trembling with concern.

Holly slowly stood up, brushed off her red dress, grabbed her matching red purse, and awkwardly put on the shoes that had flown in different directions. Though the children were worried, Holly was determined to make it to church.

Later that day, when they returned home, Holly was in too

much pain to prepare dinner. She went to bed, and was grateful that she was saved from what could have been a much worse fall. But her struggles only seemed to intensify. She groaned and clutched her stomach as she bent over in agony. Then, she let out a heavy sigh.

She collapsed onto her knees and started to cry again. The emotional and physical pain was too much to bear. Her knees ached, and her eyes were swollen, heavy like rain clouds ready to burst. Holly felt trapped, especially as an immigrant in a foreign country, unable to find a way out.

Bang! Bang!

Her daughters knocked on her bedroom door.

"Mom, we're sorry to disturb you," one of them said softly. "But we can't let you keep doing this to yourself. We're going to the movies. So, get ready, and we are not taking no for an answer."

Knowing their mother's vulnerability, they teased her. "Mom, we're going to quit college, stay home, and wallow in self-pity like you!"

Holly slowly turned to the right and smiled. "Okay, okay, you got me." Soon, it was theme park after theme park.

"Hey, Mom!" Paula was excited to share their plan to visit Six Flags in New Jersey. Between Uber rides and the theme parks, plus helping people in her community, Holly barely had a moment to think.

Then the phone calls started again. Ring after ring, it

echoed through the quiet. "Pick up your phone," the ringtone droned on, over and over, until suddenly, there was silence. Holly sighed in relief. Even the smallest sound or sliver of light made her head throb. She went to her room, shut herself in the darkness, and took three migraine pills.

But the phone rang again and again. She wondered who really needed her attention this time, hoping it wasn't an emergency. Holly went to the living room to answer the phone. It was her daughter calling. Earlier, Holly had taken her to a recital and asked her older sister to pick her up. Holly suddenly realized it had been an hour and a half late, and her daughter was in a bad neighborhood where something terrible could happen. She could even get raped. Quickly, she grabbed her keys and purse and rushed out the door.

When she got to the car, she noticed she wasn't dressed appropriately. She looked down at herself as she was still battling the pulsating headache. When she arrived at the destination, her daughter was nowhere to be seen. She called her cellphone but got no answer. Holly began to panic as confusion settled in. So she called her eldest daughter to check if she had picked up her sister.

"No, Mom. Do you want me to call the police?"

Quickly, Holly replied, "No."

She got out of her car, scanned the area, and decided to give her daughter one more call. This time, the call was picked up.

"Samantha, where the hell are you?" Holly yelled in a worrying voice.

"Mom, I'm inside. I got scared, so I stayed indoors," her daughter replied calmly as she realized how worried her mom was. "I'm coming out now."

As soon as Samantha stepped outside, Holly rushed to hug and kiss her. "Let's get out of here. Let's go."

They drove in silence for a while.

"Mom, can you get me something to drink? I'm really thirsty," Samantha asked, finally breaking the ice.

Holly looked at her daughter, smiled softly, and, in a quiet voice, said, "Sweetheart, can you wait until we get home?" She then reached over, brushed Samantha's hair back, and kissed her forehead.

"Okay, Mom," Samantha agreed.

As soon as they got home, Holly made sure her daughter had something to eat and drink. But just as she settled down, the phone rang again. She picked up the call, only to be greeted with a panicked voice from the other end of the line.

"Holly! Oh, Holly! My son!" It was her sister from Canada, and she was frantic.

Holly tried to speak, but her sister didn't give her a chance. "I rushed him to the ER, and no one has even tried to see him! I've been here for almost two days, and my son is still in my arms!" she cried.

"What's going on?!" Holly shouted, trying to get a word in.

"Sis, my son is dying!" her sister choked out before abruptly hanging up.

Holly's nephew, Jordon, was only 16 months old. He had started walking at six months. By the time he turned one, he knew the alphabet and could count to twenty, even turning on the TV to watch his favorite show. Holly was in disbelief as she tried to comprehend what was happening.

The next day, Holly called her sister again to check on the situation. "Sis, did the doctors finally help him?" she asked anxiously.

"No, the doctor at the hospital told me to take him home because he was 'healthy,'" Her sister replied. Holly could sense from her sister's voice that she was almost on the verge of crying. "Sis, all the other white children were seen except mine. I cried and begged them for 24 hours, but they didn't care. So I took him to our private doctor. The moment he saw Jordon, he yelled at me and said, 'Don't you see the baby is dying? Have you taken him to a hospital?!'"

Holly dropped to the floor and cried along with her sister.

Right then, her sister hung up and told her she was getting a call from the private doctor. After gathering the necessary information from the first hospital, the private doctor made an urgent call to another facility. "Get him there as fast as you can," the doctor instructed Holly's sister.

Holly's sister drove through every traffic light. Her foot was pressed hard on the pedal. What should have taken ten minutes took her only four. When she finally arrived at the Children's ER on the seventh floor, there were no doctors or nurses - just a trainee who had no experience and was visibly scared when she saw the baby.

Holly's sister screamed and pleaded with her to call a doctor. When the doctor finally arrived and saw the child's condition, he immediately requested a stretcher. But it took too long; there was a severe shortage of staff.

Holly's sister held her baby close and desperately tried to do something... anything to make him look lively again. She pressed her cheek to her son's cold forehead, whispering frantically, "Stay with me. Please, baby, don't leave me. Not now..." She continuously cradled him before the doctor returned with some assistance. By then, the baby was on the brink of his final breath.

"Please hurry," she urged as her voice broke. "He's going to die."

The doctor and staff initially dismissed her urgency, assuming she was just panicking, not knowing she was a nurse. Her mind raced as her heart broke. *How can they stand there, moving so slowly?* She wanted to scream at them, shake them, beg them to understand that time was slipping away. *Is it because he's colored? Would they have rushed if he were white?*

Finally, the doctor laid the child on the stretcher and began hooking up the IV, but it was too late. Before they could finish, Holly's nephew stretched out his tiny body one last time and took his final breath.

"No!" Holly's sister screamed as her heart shattered into a million pieces. The pain was unbearable, raw, and consuming. She lunged toward her son, but a nurse grabbed her, holding her back.

"Let them do their job," the nurse said softly, but it was useless. The job should have been done hours ago. *Why did it take this long?* Her son was gone.

Holly cried for days. Guilt and sorrow wrapped around her chest like a heavy chain. She could only listen to her sister's grief through the phone, powerless to console her, separated by distance and helplessness. She wanted to be there for her, to hold her, to share in the burden of her loss. But all she could do was sob into her pillow, haunted by the fact that her nephew had been treated differently because he was biracial – half white and half black.

Days turned into a blur of heartache. Holly's thoughts spiraled into misery. *Why is it always those who deserve help the least that get it the quickest? Why did this happen to him… to us?*

Holly thought that her reason for living seemed to have flown out of the window, replaced by a deep, painful void. Every morning, she would sit by the window and watch the sun rise slowly into the sky. She envied the birds as they flitted joyfully through the trees, chirping in the breeze as their wings carried them wherever they pleased. She sighed as her gaze dawdled on the green trees. She felt disconnected from the world's beauty as if happiness existed in a place she could no longer reach.

Chapter 6: The Black Rose - Romantic Interlude

It had been a year, and Holly and her daughters were back in college. The struggle was still real, but Holly had gotten used to living with the pressure. Samantha, now in her sophomore year, had learned not to bother her mom for anything unnecessary. She returned home for spring break, and now it was time to head back to campus.

"Mom, let's load everything into the car tonight so we don't have to rush in the morning!" Samantha's voice was full of excitement since she was very eager to return to school. Holly nodded and masked the exhaustion she felt. They packed up everything that night, trying to keep the mood light. The next morning, they left at 3 a.m., hoping to beat the traffic and reach their destination early.

When they finally arrived, the rain began to pour down in heavy sheets. Holly and Samantha sat in the car for a while, both avoiding the goodbye. The windshield wipers moved back and forth, clearing the rain in motion. Holly felt reality sinking in. She helped her daughter move everything into her dorm and arranged her room, making sure Samantha was settled and comfortable before leaving.

Holly drove away with the same ache in her heart. The pit in her stomach grew tighter with every mile she put between them. *How am I going to pay her school fees this time?* The thoughts swirled in her mind. No matter how hard she tried, the burden always seemed too big to bear.

Suddenly, her phone rang and interrupted her spiraling thoughts. Holly glanced at the screen and saw her best friend's name flash across it. She hesitated for a moment, then answered.

"Hi, hi… Ah, hi," Holly stuttered as she tried to find words but failed to piece them together.

"Where are you?" her friend asked casually.

"I'm in New York," Holly replied.

"Okay. Why don't you stop by? I'll pay for you to stay overnight at the Sheraton Hotel," he offered.

Holly sat in her car, silent for what felt like an eternity. Her mind raced and battled with the decision in front of her. She knew what this invitation really meant. It wasn't just about a hotel room. It never was. Her stomach twisted with unease.

"Okay, sure," Holly finally replied. As she ended the call, her heart skipped a beat. Her hands gripped the steering wheel so tightly that her knuckles became white.

What am I doing? she thought. She knew she was walking into something she didn't want, something she had promised herself she would never do. Yet, here she was… trapped by her own impulses.

She stared at the road ahead, rain still pouring down, and felt trapped. Once again, she had traded a piece of her dignity for survival. *Is this what my life has come to?*

As soon as she entered the driveway of the Sheraton Hotel, there he was, holding a bouquet of roses, waving and blowing kisses at her. Holly parked by the entrance as he took the car keys, handed her the flowers, kissed her, and then drove off to park the car. Zahir was excited to see her, while Holly stood with mixed emotions, knowing he was a married man. When he returned, he grabbed her around the waist and lifted her into the air. Holly lost her balance, but he caught her, which brought them face-to-face. Their eyes locked. He gently raised her and planted a kiss on her that lasted nearly a minute. Holly was swayed by him, her mouth slightly ajar, her beautiful, shining eyes staring deep into his eyes.

Zahir quickly set her down and said, "Lady D! Please watch your step." They giggled as they walked together. All this time, his arm was tightly wrapped around her waist.

Holly was surprised by the effort he had put into decorating the room. The bed was covered in red and white rose petals arranged in a heart shape, and the pathway was lined with white petals. There was champagne, which confused Holly, as she knew he couldn't drink alcohol. However, she decided not to spoil the moment. Zahir playfully lifted her and threw her onto the bed. Then he told her to close her eyes. Holly, though perplexed, obeyed, even though she didn't like surprises. He handed her a box. Inside was the most beautiful red dress Holly had ever seen, along with another small box containing a pair of diamond earrings and a matching necklace.

"Get dressed, my lady. We're going out," he said.

Holly took a shower and then remembered she only had a pair of sneakers. "Sneakers with such a fancy dress and these diamonds?" She chuckled to herself and got ready. She carefully combed her hair and applied a little makeup. Zahir stood still, radiantly gazing at her. She could feel his eyes undressing her. Holly walked over and put on her sneakers, and Zahir burst into laughter. He laughed and laughed. He was handsomely dressed in a black suit, a purple shirt, and a striking necklace.

"Lady D, I have something else for you. Here are your shoes," he said, bending down to place them on her feet. "Ah, there you are. Now you have a sense of class."

Holly smiled, knowing he had a good sense of humor. He took her to the Metropolitan Opera House. Though he wasn't a fan of opera, he knew it was one of Holly's dreams. Holly was speechless as her emotions were soaring. As they sat down, he rested her head on his shoulder, but Holly couldn't stay still. She had forgotten about her daughter's school fees and all the worries that had burdened her. She held onto his hands tightly as he kissed them over and over.

After the show, they ended the evening with a dinner waiting for them back at the hotel. Zahir, knowing she was prepared to stay, had bought her sexy lace lingerie. That night, they tangled with each other in moans and groans, tossing and turning through several positions, climaxing over and over. The next morning, they were exhausted, barely able to move, and still breathless.

Eventually, Holly returned to reality and told him she had to leave. She set aside the Cinderella-like fantasy, put back on her dirty, sweaty clothes and sneakers, and rushed out of the hotel. Zahir chased after her. Before she could close the car door, he pulled it open. "Please, don't do this again," he pleaded. "Anyway, take this and drive carefully." He handed her a bag filled with everything he had bought her, along with an envelope of money.

Halfway through her drive, her phone rang. Holly got frustrated because she couldn't navigate without her GPS and didn't know how to switch between calls and maps easily. She decided to answer the phone. It was Zahir.

Trying not to sound annoyed, she softened her tone. "Hi, sweetheart, how are you?"

"Did you look in the bag I gave you?" he asked. Holly, confused but curious, reached over to grab the bag from the passenger seat. Inside, she found a large sum of money stacked in hundred-dollar bills. Zahir knew that if he had handed it to her directly, she would have refused it.

She called him back and thanked him. As fantasy and reality clashed, her religious beliefs haunted her. Still, Holly smiled.

Chapter 7: The Power of the Heart

Later that evening, Holly had a cup of tea with toast and two over-easy eggs.

She sat on the balcony, staring at the sky, when she heard, "Mummy! Mummy!"

She turned and saw her daughter, Paula, who had recently returned to continue her studies at UDC. 'I couldn't afford to help her,' Holly thought to herself.

"Mummy, you have an interview!" Paula said excitedly.

Holly turned around and replied, "Child, calm down." She looked at Paula's overly amused face and read the email.

"Dear Holly, you are scheduled for an interview…" The email continued, and Holly saw light at the end of the tunnel. She smiled as she recalled her two daughters' accomplishments in university.

'Sometimes a mom has to do what a mom has to do. Hey, don't judge me,' Holly thought. She had given up her career to make sure her children didn't suffer as she had. Suddenly, she felt a sense of pride in her children's achievements and hoped that she, too, would taste that glory. She thought that building self-confidence, feeling love, and experiencing happiness were her successes.

Seven months later, Holly quit her job at the postal service and embraced a new challenge at another company. Her confidence and poise quickly led her to become a manager.

Exercising and jogging became new hobbies for her. She sat on a bench in the park, tilting her head back as the wind blew her hair gently. Holly smiled and brushed her hair back. Finally, she was letting go and savoring life. Her self-esteem was no longer tied to what others thought of her. She stood up and began to twirl around with her arms wide open. She spun and spun until she lost her balance and fell softly to the grass. Lying on her back, she gazed up at the sky and closed her eyes for a brief moment until she felt a shadow pass over her.

She slowly opened one eye, and there, looming over her, was a man. Holly quickly scrambled to her feet as he extended a hand to help her up. She refused and stood up. Then, she asked, "And who are you?!"

The man apologized and introduced himself. Holly was slightly irritated. She wasn't looking for love - she'd given up on that. All she wanted was to be happy and embrace her life as it was.

"My name is Ethan. I just wanted to say hi," he said.

Out of politeness, Holly extended her hand. To her surprise, he lifted it, kissed it, and said, "Pleased to meet you."

Before she could say another word, he walked away. Holly stared after him, shrugged, and laughed. 'Oh well then,' she said to herself and laughed uncontrollably. To her, this was just another joke or another man trying to mess up her life.

Holly was now happy again. She bought herself an ice cream cone and licked it quickly to keep it from melting all over her hands. She skipped and twirled occasionally as she wandered through the park. She watched couples kissing, holding hands, and relaxing on the grass, giggling at the sight of children playing nearby. The wind blew up her short dress, and she bent down gently to keep it from flying up. Unbeknownst to her, Ethan was watching from a distance and chuckled to himself.

"Hmmm, sexy," he muttered as he seemed clearly amused by this carefree woman. The more he watched her, the more intrigued he became. Ethan's curiosity got the better of him - he wanted to meet her again. He asked one of his guards to follow her and gather as much information as possible.

Meanwhile, Holly went over to the fountain for a drink of water. Her hair fell over her face and got soaked. As she tried to push it back, she heard a voice behind her.

"Madam, is your hair in the way?"

She lifted her head and blew her hair back with a smile. "It's okay," she replied. The man stood there, watching her. Holly felt uneasy and was about to snap at him when he interrupted.

"Mam, the gentleman would like to know your name."

"What gentleman?" Holly asked.

"Across the lawn, to your left."

Realizing the conversation was going nowhere, the man walked away. Ethan, having learned her full name, decided that was enough for now.

Ethan planned a black-and-white masquerade party and invited Holly's best friend, Terry, making sure she would convince Holly to attend. At first, it was difficult to persuade Holly. But Terry persisted, and eventually, Holly gave in. The idea of being disguised intrigued her, so she went shopping for the occasion.

That night, Holly wore a long, white pencil dress that accentuated her slender figure. She completed the look with a white feathered mask and silver 12-inch heels. Terry complimented Holly on her appearance, but Holly dismissed it.

"Terry, you're just saying that to make me feel good. By the way, that's what friends are for," she joked.

Holly chuckled and said, "Let's go before I change my mind."

As Holly reached the entrance of the ballroom, the guests turned and began to gossip, wondering who she was. Ethan had been trying desperately to find Holly but had failed. He noticed a lady dressed in white but was afraid to approach her. Yet, he felt inexplicably drawn to her. Everywhere Holly went, his eyes followed her. His conversations with the guests became so distracted that they started asking if he was okay. His father noticed his strange behavior and inquired about what was going on.

Ethan finally recognized Terry when she removed her mask. He quickly approached her and asked if Holly was there. Terry nodded, smiled, and pointed in Holly's direction.

"Ethan, you owe me one," Terry called out.

Ethan walked up to Holly and asked for a dance. She hesitated, then bowed and nodded. As she began to walk gingerly across the dance floor, he placed one hand around her waist and held her hand with the other. She rested her left hand on his shoulder as they waltzed onto the floor. He turned her, and soon, they were dancing cheek to cheek.

Holly missed a step, which caused her mask to slip slightly. That moment revealed her light brown, glassy eyes. She tried to adjust it and hoped he wouldn't notice, but Ethan whispered her name. Her eyes led him to her heart. Holly cleared her throat. Right then, Ethan let go of her and said, "Shall we?"

After dancing for what felt like a fleeting moment, Ethan felt the heat between them intensify. His heart was pounding, not from the physical exertion of dancing but from the thrill of being so close to her.

"How about we take a walk?" Ethan suggested, his voice barely cutting through the noise of the room. He was craving a moment alone with her, a chance to escape the crowded dance floor and the eyes of everyone around them. He needed space, space to breathe, and space to unravel the mystery that seemed to surround her.

Holly hesitated for just a second, then smiled and nodded in agreement. They both excused themselves from the dance floor. The cool air hit them the moment they stepped outside. The night was crisp, the sky above speckled with stars, and for a brief moment, they stood in silence as if both were trying to collect their thoughts.

"Can I get you a drink?" Ethan offered, breaking the silence. He was used to being in control, used to reading people easily, but she was different. There was something about her - something he couldn't quite put his finger on - that intrigued him. It wasn't just her beauty; it was the way she carried herself, the quiet confidence that radiated from her.

She shook her head gently, a small smile tugging at the corners of her lips. "No, thank you," she replied. Ethan thought that now he had the chance to learn more about the woman who made his heart race… or so he thought.

Ethan's friend watched and grew jealous. Just as Ethan was about to ask Holly out on a date, his phone rang. He checked the caller ID, sighed, and muttered under his breath, "Damn it." Ethan smiled, but before he could apologize, Holly said she had to go. Ethan reached out, gently held her upper arm, and tugged her closer. They found themselves facing each other, locked in deep eye contact. Holly was speechless. Quickly, she pulled away and ran off to the car park.

Ethan, a Caucasian man with greenish-hazel eyes, stood six and a half feet tall with a muscular build. He had a charismatic personality and a hint of childish behavior. He enjoyed working out in his gym and jogging before starting his busy day. Holly couldn't stop thinking about his seductive smile, his physique, and the way he dressed. She sat in her car, speeding away as she tried to escape her feelings. She didn't even think about the friend who had brought her to the party.

In fact, she felt like she had been set up.

"This cannot happen!" she screamed as she pounded the steering wheel over and over again.

Ethan couldn't sleep that night. He tossed and turned as his imagination ran wild. He got up and had a drink, but it didn't help. He turned on the television and flipped from one channel to another. Suddenly, his mother walked into his room after returning from a long vacation in the Bahamas. As they chatted, she noticed the look of confusion and happiness that seemed to consume him.

"So, who's the lucky one?" she asked without hesitation.

"Pardon me?"

"Who is the lucky girl?" she asked with a knowing smile. Ethan smirked, but before he could describe Holly, his brother Zahir walked in and greeted their mother with a kiss on the forehead.

He turned to Ethan and asked, "And who is this girl?"

Ethan walked away in anger. The two brothers had never gotten along since their father died. Ethan walked to the garden and thought and talked to himself.

The next day was Monday. Ethan was in a business meeting, but all he could think about was how he could sway Holly so that he could express his feelings to her. The meeting was going on, but his mind was distracted. Eventually, the meeting ended, and as he was about to leave, his brother greeted him with a huge smile on his face. How could he express his love for Holly to a brother he wanted to be close to yet felt so distant from? A brother he hated yet yearned to love? Their father had wished for them to be close before he died. Ethan put his personal feelings aside to accommodate his brother, trying to suppress his hatred and anger in a hypocritical way.

"As you can see, the business is finally moving in the right direction," Ethan said, forcing a smile.

"Brother, I'm not here to discuss business. I want you to be the best man at my wedding," Zahir replied. He got up, smirked at his brother, and as he walked away, he called out his engagement party date, saying he wanted Ethan to be there.

"Aren't you married?" Ethan asked.

"Brother, I met the lady of my dreams, and I'm planning on getting a divorce," Zahir said and continued to walk away with a smile. Ethan's stomach churned. He felt sick to the core.

***

The very next day, Holly took an early morning jog. As she closed her eyes to stretch her upper arms, she was startled by a towel being handed to her. Holly stuttered as her heart raced in her chest. "Not again!" she exclaimed, bending forward and holding her knees. Ethan offered her a bottle of water. She looked up, only to be faced with his now hazel eyes. Ethan helped her stand and asked if she was okay. Holly's heart gave way, and Ethan caught her. He gently kissed her on the lips, hoping to send the right message. After a few minutes,

Holly was back on her feet. She ran her finger over her lips and tried to savor the moment but was interrupted.

"Is everything okay with your lips?" Ethan asked with a childish smile as he walked away slowly.

Holly watched him leave, then jogged back to the villa that had been left to Zahir after their father's death. Holly's daughter had just graduated from college, and she decided to buy a house and add her daughter to the title. Excitement filled her when Holly was approved for a loan to purchase the home of her dreams. A week later, she got a call from the loan officer.

"Holly, I need your divorce decree so that I can finalize the details," the officer said.

Holly became upset and raised her voice. She remembered how she had been thrown out of the house she bought.

"You dirty, good-for-nothing idiot! Take your cursed children and leave this property right now!" her ex-husband had shouted. "You're too pretty, and all men want to do is get you into their beds. No one wants you." He had dragged her to the gate by her hair and spat in her face, then began unzipping his pants. "You're so good in bed! I'm going to give you this today!" he had sneered. Holly had screamed at the top of her lungs.

"Stop, please stop!" He had punched her several times in the face. Her nose started to bleed, and her eyes were swollen and covered with blood. She could hardly see. He had licked her tears as he tried to rip her clothes off.

"You drive me crazy!" he had said as he forced himself into her mouth. Holly had bitten down hard, gnawing at him as if she were

circumcising him with her teeth. He had grabbed his bloody organ and then kicked and punched her mercilessly.

"You jerk!!! This isn't over," he had shouted.

Breaking away from her attacker, Holly wiped the blood from her eyes, picked up the plastic bags containing her children's clothes, and fought to get the keys to release her children, who had been locked inside the house.

Holly shook her head, snapping back to the present as the loan officer continued asking questions about her divorce.

"That's one major déjà vu," she muttered. "Oh, not you," she added, smiling as she explained that she had not received a penny from the divorce. At the end of the phone call, she asked the officer to email her all the necessary documents. Surprisingly, everything went well, and she moved into her dream house along with her daughter, Samantha.

Holly's company was expanding their business, focusing on New York, and Holly wanted to be in charge of the project. It was her chance to showcase her expertise in finding the right spot, negotiating, and signing contracts. After her presentation, the CEO decided she was the best candidate. Holly called Zahir for help.

"Zahir, I need your help. I know you're a prominent realtor, and you have strong connections," she said.

Zahir listened, then asked, "What's in it for me?"

"Remember, I promised to marry you as soon as you get your..."

"Holly, no one should know about you. I told my brother I'm engaged just to make him jealous," Zahir interrupted.

"Okay, well, grant me this one favor," Holly said as she explained what she was looking for in terms of price and location. In less than a month, the company was preparing to take over another firm by purchasing two twin buildings on either side of it, which was a major move. The company praised Holly by throwing a party in her honor. It was becoming increasingly difficult for men to resist her; Holly had developed a strong sense of self-esteem. Her personality shone through in the way she walked, talked, and smiled. The overwhelming attention prompted her to talk it over with her best friend, Kay, a psychologist specializing in sex addiction.

Holly called Kay and asked if she could spend the weekend with her. After revealing everything that had been happening and how men seemed to become addicted to her, especially if they slept with her, Kay's interest was piqued. After a couple of sessions, Kay stopped and asked, "What kind of magic do you have down there?!"

Holly was shocked. "What the hell are you talking about?"

Kay explained that Holly seemed to have an 'unbridled gratification' that produced an 'unbridled desire' in men. She went on to say that some women possess a kind of allure that acts like a powerful magnet that draws men in irresistibly.

"What do you mean?" Holly asked. She was clearly perplexed.

Kay smiled and then replied, "This type has the same effect as a mouth. You're one lucky woman, blessed with inner and outer beauty, a powerful charm, and the ability to satisfy all your lover's sexual desires."

Holly felt both shocked and intrigued. She wondered if this was a good thing or bad. Kay explained how she could control her libido and suggested activities that could help.

Meanwhile, Ethan hired a detective to find out where Holly hung out and where she lived. Holly's distant relationship with Zahir sometimes led her to seek fulfillment elsewhere. One evening, Holly returned home from a meeting and was super exhausted. She flicked off her shoes as soon as she stepped inside, stripped, and stood in the shower for a while. Afterward, she slipped into a white negligee, poured herself a drink, and turned on the television as she absentmindedly flipped through Tinder. Suddenly, there was a knock on her door.

She called out to Samantha, asking if she was expecting any guests, and asked her to answer the door since she was trying to get some time to herself.

Samantha called back, "Mom, Mom!!! Oh, Mom, he's so hot and sexy!"

"What are you talking about?" Holly asked, rising to see who it was, only to be greeted by Ethan standing in her living room.

"Holly, it's a pleasure to meet you. I couldn't help

myself… I was in the neighborhood and decided to stop by and say hi."

"I see, and now you're standing here in my…" Holly trailed off, struggling to find the words to accommodate a friend, though it was clear he was more than just a friend of interest.

Ethan turned the tables on her, using reverse psychology. "Gosh, you're beautiful, but your attitude stinks. I thought you were someone of grace, a lady of virtue, but I was wrong."

With that, Ethan slammed the door and left. Holly's ego was immediately sparked. "Who the hell does he think he is, slamming my door and walking out on me? I'm going to show him who I am," she thought.

Holly opened the door and ran after him. When Ethan turned around, all he could see was her slender beauty, her hair bouncing in the air like droplets of diamonds as she floated closer to him. Holly stopped, looked up into his deep blue eyes, and gave him a kiss that weakened his knees. Then, without another word, she let him go and walked back into her house.

Ethan smiled and muttered to himself, "Oh yes!" He tugged at his jacket, licked his lips, and drove off in his Maserati.

Chapter 8: Presenter REAI

Zahir had just perfected his real estate broker hologram, a project he'd been working on since he was seventeen. Growing up, he always had a passion for financing, investments, and developing buildings, especially using materials indigenous to each country. As he advanced in the field of real estate, he created an app to streamline and optimize the development process, which he named REAI (Real Estate Artificial Intelligence).

REAI could accurately design a building, identify available properties, and provide insights on when to buy or sell. It could even detect a buyer's or seller's mood, gauge their readiness to make a deal and suggest the best companies for a client to work with. Zahir's technology placed him at the top of his field, which allowed him to communicate with REAI through text or voice commands. He also developed contact lenses and glasses that enabled him to see and hear the holographic data that REAI provided. The technology was versatile and allowed the user to customize the hologram's appearance. However, only the user could see the image.

If Zahir had to travel to another country, he could decode REAI for added security. It also had the ability to detect hacking attempts and would automatically enter a protective mode, rebuilding and rebooting itself as needed.

Zahir saw REAI as a way to strengthen his bond with his brother by helping him gain more investors and make savvy stock market investments. Recognizing Holly's expertise from their previous collaborations, Zahir decided to involve her in assisting Ethan with REAI for a major future merger.

As summer began, everyone around was busy decorating; flowers were blooming, and lawns were neatly manicured. That morning, Holly woke up in her white negligee, stretched, and walked to the kitchen to make herself a cup of tea. She moved toward the glass door that led to her balcony, opened it, and felt the wind catch the outer sheer of her negligee. Her hair bounced along with the wind. After taking another sip of tea, she placed the cup on a glass coffee table and stepped out onto the balcony. She stretched her hands upward and took a deep breath, whispering to herself, "Gosh, Ethan is driving me crazy."

Just then, her phone rang. Holly went to her room to retrieve it, only to see that she had missed a call from Zahir.

"Zahir, hey, good morning. How can I help you?" Holly sat on the edge of the bed, crossing her legs.

"So, what are you wearing?" Zahir asked playfully. Holly started reminiscing about the few times they had met as Zahir continued to talk about those moments as if they were happening now. She shook her head, stood up, and walked toward the kitchen.

"So... you didn't call me for this, did you?"

"Come on, don't be crazy now. You know you want me, and you miss me!" Zahir joked, spinning around in his chair and teasing his hair.

"Zahir, what do you need? If you don't tell me, I'm going to hang up this phone."

"Hmm, sassy today, I love that. Girl, you're on fire!" Zahir sensed that Holly wasn't in the mood for games, so he got to the point. "Okay then, remember you promised one."

"Yep, okay, what is it you want this time?"

Holly and Zahir had worked on many projects together, apart from the one he had helped her with for her company.

"Holly, I have a project I want you to help me with for another company. I promised to pay you well - just name your price, and it's yours," Zahir said. He explained the type of materials she'd be working with and those he'd bring to her.

Holly was excited; this was her area of expertise. Not only that, but Zahir was a great mentor. The room fell silent, except for a few quiet giggles. Zahir then provided the company's name, its goals, and the team of managers she'd be meeting with.

After the call with Holly, Zahir called Ethan, and the two discussed the necessary details. During their first meeting, Zahir and Ethan briefly talked about the project, but Zahir never disclosed who would be handling the programming or presenting it to investors.

The next morning, Holly woke up early, agonizing over what to wear. This was her first time meeting a millionaire, along with his executive board and managers. It took her two hours to choose the right outfit and another two hours for her makeup.

Holly finally settled on a burgundy leather skirt and matching jacket. The skirt had a slit running from her knee to mid-thigh. She wore a sheer blouse that hugged her body but wasn't too revealing, paired with burgundy heels that showed off her freshly manicured nails.

She called an Uber, which took her to the meeting. Stepping out of the car, she clutched her beige bag, then slung it over her shoulder. She straightened her posture and walked confidently to the front desk, asking for the conference room on the 10th floor.

As the elevator doors opened, she saw the conference room directly ahead. Inside, some of the men were on their phones, checking their watches, reading, or chatting with one another. Holly was feeling prepared. She walked in gracefully, smiled, and greeted them in their respective languages.

The men exchanged glances and chatted briefly before falling silent. Ethan, the CEO of the company, entered right behind her and moved beside her, curious to see who his brother had recommended for the meeting.

Holly glanced at him and tucked her hair behind her ear. Their eyes met and locked; both were momentarily struck silent. Holly felt her heart racing and her chest tightening. Now, she was feeling lightheaded. Just as she was about to faint, Ethan caught her and laid her gently on the table.

The men cheered Ethan on for his quick thinking. Ethan stroked Holly's hair, and as he leaned closer to her lips, she slapped him. Clearing his throat, he said, "I see you're feeling better now." The men laughed again.

Ethan helped her up, and after a few quick words, they were prepared to begin the presentation. The deadline was tight, and Ethan needed to present the project to his investors that day. After the presentation, the managers and executive board members met with the investors in another room. Following an intense period of listening and nodding, the investors signed the contract, signaling their approval.

Holly couldn't wait to leave. She was confused - how did Zahir know Ethan? She hurried into the elevator, closing her eyes and exhaling loudly.

Meanwhile, Ethan instructed the building's engineer to stop the elevator on the next floor. As the doors opened on the ninth floor, Holly opened her eyes, expecting someone to get in. When the doors wouldn't close, she pressed the buttons repeatedly in frustration. Giving up, she decided to take the stairs.

The moment she stepped out, someone grabbed her arm. She tried to pull away but couldn't deny her feelings. Ethan pulled her back into the elevator, and as the doors closed, he gently lifted her chin, locking his gaze with her hungry eyes.

Ethan wanted Holly to need him as much as he needed her. He moved closer and closer, watching her lips tremble and her body practically begging for him. He pressed his lips against hers as his fingers traced up the inside of her thigh. Clothes quickly began to come off, but Ethan suddenly stopped, realizing the engineer was likely watching. They both hurriedly dressed.

Ethan sighed, then asked, "Would you like to come to the penthouse with me?"

Holly composed herself and replied, "Maybe next time," still confused about everything that had happened.

Ethan drove her home and kissed her goodnight. That night, Holly tossed and turned, puzzled by the thought that Ethan and Zahir didn't look alike. She began to question whether they could really be brothers. Ethan, too, was unsettled, especially wondering how Zahir knew about his girlfriend. Jealousy burned inside him, and anger toward his brother led him to a dark place.

Early the next morning, Holly called Zahir. He sounded excited to hear from her, eager to share the success of the business deal.

"Zahir, where do you know Ethan from?" Holly asked in a tense voice.

Sensing something was wrong, Zahir asked, "Did the presentation go well?"

Trying to remain calm, Holly responded, "Yes, the presentation went very well. The investors signed the contract that day."

"That's great!" Zahir said, clearly pleased. He'd been

hoping to reconnect with his brother.

"So, Zahir, where do you know Ethan from?" she pressed.

"Holly, he's my brother."

"Brother?!?" Holly repeated, stunned.

Zahir noticed a change in her tone and pretended not to notice. He asked casually, "Are you okay?"

"Oh, yeah," Holly replied, trying to sound nonchalant.

Zahir excused himself, saying he had another call. Holly panicked and quickly asked him not to mention anything to Ethan until she sorted things out. Zahir agreed though Holly was now left wondering: did Zahir know about Ethan? Did Ethan know about Zahir? Could she be getting played by both brothers?

To clear her head, Holly went for a jog in the park. She knew she was in love with Ethan, but Zahir was her best friend. His friendship meant a lot to her, and although they had shared romantic moments, it hadn't affected their bond.

Holly spread a towel on the grass, lay down in the sun, and slipped on her sunglasses, wishing for answers. A shadow passed over her, and when she looked up, she saw Ethan standing there.

"So, this is one of your 'getaway' moments, huh?" he teased, crouching down with one leg on either side of her, leaving her with little room to move. Though she loved him, the fear of loving and losing him seemed too much. If the earth could swallow her whole, she thought, life would be much simpler.

Holly sat up quickly, accidentally bumping Ethan in the nose, knocking him flat on his back. She panicked and leaned over to check if he was hurt. Ethan, however, tugged at her hand, causing her to lose balance and fall on top of him. What started as an attempt to resist turned into playful rolling and kissing.

Finally, Ethan had her pinned to the ground, both of them breathing heavily. After a moment, he got up and offered her his hand. Holly took the opportunity to grab her towel and sprint away. Ethan stood there, astonished.

"Damn it! Why does this woman always run?" he muttered, but secretly, it gave him all the more reason to chase her. She made him feel alive, and for the first time, he realized he was falling in love.

Ethan had never been in love before. He'd had plenty of women, selecting them by occupation, by race, and by whatever else struck his fancy. He'd always believed no man should settle, thinking that there were too many fish in the sea. "Why eat steak every day?" he'd joke to his friends.

But they always told him, "When you find the one, you'll know."

These thoughts swirled in Ethan's mind as he found himself chasing after a woman who kept running away from him. What he felt for Holly seemed different to him.

When he finally caught up to her, he grabbed her arm, turned her around, and asked, "Holly, can we talk for a moment? Gosh!"

Holly nodded, and they sat under a tree overlooking a pond.

"Can you tell me why you keep running away from me?" he asked, turning to meet her gaze. Holly kept her head down, unable to accept that someone like Ethan could truly like her… maybe even love her.

She raised her head and asked, "Okay, tell me three things you like about yourself and three things you dislike."

Ethan chuckled. "Are you serious?"

They both laughed, sharing personal thoughts back and forth like they were syncing up. "Me too, me too!" they exclaimed, holding hands as if their minds had aligned.

"Nah, no way… we're both scared to love," Ethan said, making them both laugh harder. Neither of them was ready for the intensity of their connection, but they couldn't deny that it was there.

Ethan suddenly stopped laughing and gently ran his hand along her cheek. He tilted her head up as if to kiss her, but then both of their phones rang. Ethan resisted the urge to answer, letting it ring as he leaned in. Right then, Holly found herself locked in a passionate kiss as her body gave in; they were devouring each other without restraint.

"Holly," Ethan moaned. "Can I take you home?"

The question broke the moment. Holly pulled back, holding his face close as tears welled in her eyes. "I can't resist you. Everything in me is drawn to you. You… your words… your touch… you're like a volcano ready to erupt after being dormant for years."

Ethan looked deeply into her eyes, wiping her tears away. "Holly, just let go. Let me love you. I can't see my life without you. I'm empty inside without you."

He had never been more vulnerable, but all Holly could do was run away again. Ethan was dazed. He called one of his security guards and asked him to take her home.

Back at his own place, Ethan couldn't focus on work. He lay down, got up again, poured himself a glass of water, and paced the room. Meanwhile, Holly showered, slipped into a silky negligee, and waited. She stared at her phone, hoping it would ring, but sleep eluded her. She tossed and turned, finally throwing a pillow against the wall.

"I'm such a coward. Damn it! Damnnn it!!!"

Ethan, having instructed his guard to leave her door open, quietly entered her room and stood in the dark, watching her toss and turn. Unable to bear it any longer, he stepped outside and called her.

Holly answered immediately. "I'm outside your door. Can you please let me in?"

Without hesitation, Holly ran to the door and leaped into his arms. Ethan carried her to the bedroom and pleasured her as their bodies entwined and gave in to their desires. They moaned and groaned like two humans in heat. Ethan teased her, and eventually, their sheets ended up in a heap on the floor by the time they finally collapsed, exhausted.

The next morning, they woke up feeling as if they'd run a marathon. They laughed, and Ethan kissed her, whispering, "I want you to be my wife someday."

Holly was speechless. She felt overwhelmed by the turn of events.

Ethan left for work, and soon after, Zahir called. His concern for Holly's well-being only added to her confusion.

A few days later, Holly arranged to meet Zahir. He was anxious to hear how things had gone between her and his brother. Driving upstate wasn't easy for Holly, though she hated long drives, especially with her fear of trucks and nighttime lights. At 3 a.m., she set out, hoping to reach her destination by 8 a.m. With a coffee in one cup holder, a water bottle in the other, and a tuna sandwich for the road, she tried to keep herself occupied. But her mind kept drifting to the difficult conversation ahead - how would she tell Zahir that she was in love with his brother?

Her daughter Samantha had already tried to discourage her, calling her a "whore trying to break up families." Holly had spent years searching for love, and now, just as she thought she'd found it, there were barriers everywhere - societal expectations, family judgments, and her upbringing in a strict religious household where divorce and contraception were condemned.

Her mother had always warned her, "If you sleep with a married man, your womb is cursed, and your clothes will be torn to pieces."

Holly started to distract her mind to push away the guilt. At one point, the road was covered in fog, giving the landscape an eerie, ghostly feel. A certain type of fear began to creep into her mind and body.

Suddenly, she heard a horn blaring. Panicked, she hit the brakes hard. Her heart was racing frantically. She barely had time to catch her breath when-

BANG, BANG, BANG!

A loud knock startled her, coming from the window.

Holly screamed and threw her hands up in terror

Chapter 9: Breaking the Truth

"Madam, are you okay?" The voice repeated over and over until Holly responded.

"God! I'm okay, but what the hell are you doing?" Holly said in a startling tone.

"Madam, I'm the patrol police. We're here to make sure everyone gets through this fog safely. You can either pull off the road or follow behind my car."

Holly nodded.

"Madam, are you going to pull off or follow behind me?" the officer asked again.

Holly mumbled and stuttered, "I, I, I'll driiive behind yooou, officer." She waved her hand, put the car in drive, and waited for the officer to pull ahead. The unsettling moment dragged on for nearly an hour. The car was silent, which gave her an eerie feeling.

Finally, the sun began to peek out from behind the clouds and pushed the fog away. Holly thanked the officer for providing protection and continued on her journey. She booked herself into a hotel, took a hot, steamy bath, and then collapsed onto the bed, lying in a starfish position on her stomach. She screamed into the pillow. Less than a minute later, Holly was knocked out cold. It wasn't long before a message woke her.

"Meeting at 2 PM in my studio," it read.

Holly stretched, gathered herself, and then flopped back down on the bed like a teenager, hugging her pillow and thinking about Ethan. She was so in love that, on her way to Zahir's office, she found herself skipping and singing. She stopped to look at dresses on display, went inside to check the price, bought one, and hummed as she swung the bag on her arm.

Holly sat in Zahir's office for a few minutes before being greeted with a hug and a kiss. Zahir pulled back and looked at her.

"Okay! So, who's the lucky one?" he asked.

"What do you mean?" Holly asked, trying hard to hide her feelings. She had to figure out how to tell him that she was in love with his brother, hoping it wouldn't strain their friendship.

After a few hours of intense editing, Zahir decided to show off his latest creation, REIA. He handed Holly a pair of contact lenses while putting on a pair of glasses himself. He began giving commands, and Holly watched in awe.

"If you take out your contacts, you won't see or hear my display," he explained.

"Wow! You're a genius. When do you plan to release this in the field?" Holly asked, clearly amazed.

"I've tested it many times. I just need to finish some final coding."

"Zahir, do you realize what you've created?" Holly exclaimed.

"I know," he chuckled and turned off the system.

"So, back to you," Zahir said. "Who's the one?"

Holly cut in and avoided his gaze. "How's your wife?" she asked, searching for words to justify herself.

"Holly, you know I like you a lot, and I'm waiting for the divorce. But these things take time, especially when there's a lot to lose in a relationship." Zahir sighed. "As I've said before, now's not the right time. My wife will take me to the cleaners. Do you know how hard I've worked to achieve all this, just to let her claim everything?"

Zahir clenched his wine glass tightly, stood up, and stared out the window before tossing the glass to the floor.

"Zahir, calm down," Holly said in a gentle but firm tone. "As a friend, I need you to wish me well. I need to get married someday."

"Can't you wait for me?" Zahir asked in a softened voice. "I know it's been over nine years since we got close, but we've been best friends since elementary school."

"I know," Holly replied. "I've been married, divorced, married again, and now I'm a widow… and still waiting on you."

Zahir sighed deeply. "Okay… tell me. It's going to hurt, but tell me who the lucky guy is." He looked into her eyes before turning away.

"Oh, oh no! Please don't tell me… No, no, no. Gosh!

Please don't tell me you're in love with-"

Zahir walked toward her and grabbed her arms as if trying to salvage something before it was lost. Tears started streaming down Holly's rosy cheeks, making her look even more alluring as if he wanted to kiss the tears away.

Zahir's wife didn't know her husband was cheating, but he loved Holly and often told her he loved her more than his wife.

"Zahir, I didn't know!" Holly cried.

Zahir loved her so much that he'd do anything to make her happy. But this time, it was different. He wasn't going to let her go, especially not to his brother.

"Holly, I've just started rebuilding my relationship with my brother," he said, suddenly stopping mid-sentence. "Oh my God… he doesn't know."

Holly shook her head.

"Holly, let's call Ethan and discuss our meeting. We can check how the app's working for him." Before she could respond, Zahir had already started a video chat with Ethan.

"Oh, Zahir!" Ethan exclaimed excitedly. "I see you've met my beautiful future wife. By the way, how do you know her?"

Holly couldn't take the tension anymore. She grabbed her bags and bolted out of the studio. Ethan was confused by her sudden exit, but before he could ask, Zahir brusquely ended the video and ran after her.

By the time Zahir reached the ground floor, Holly was gone. She hadn't wasted any time packing and leaving the city. Now back in her car, she sped away, sobbing and occasionally banging her hand on the steering wheel.

After a long stretch of driving, she pulled over to catch her breath. All she could think about was how she'd ruined her friendship with Zahir and lost the one person who loved her so much. She got out of the car and started to sob, covering her face with both hands. Then, she held her stomach, placed her hands on her hips, and screamed at the top of her lungs.

After regaining some composure, Holly got back in the car and resumed her journey home. Her phone rang constantly - calls alternated between the brothers.

Ethan had found love, and he wasn't going to let anyone get in his way. Holly wondered what the brothers discussed after she left. When Ethan couldn't reach her, he decided to wait at her house.

As soon as Holly pulled into her driveway and got out of the car, Ethan called out to her. She ran straight into his arms. Ethan lifted her off the ground and spun her around before gently placing her down and kissing her. He cupped her cheeks in his hands and kissed her again.

"Holly, you're fucking driving me crazy. Why didn't you answer your phone?"

"Ethan, we need to talk. Let's go inside."

Holly plugged in the kettle to make tea while Ethan helped

carry her bags to the bedroom. After their tea, Holly excused herself to take a shower. She was relieved that Ethan hadn't abandoned her, and at the same time, she hoped she still had a friend in him.

Holly undressed and stepped into the shower. Ethan was unable to resist himself. He pretended to lie down but eventually got undressed and joined her. Holly couldn't see him through the steam on the glass door. Suddenly, Ethan jumped in.

"Ethan, what are you doing?" she gasped as he began to caress her breasts. The sounds of moaning under the running water and the banging against the shower glass were all that could be heard.

Ethan picked Holly up, stepped out of the shower, and tossed her onto the bed. Ethan loved creativity in the bedroom. Soon, they collapsed into climax, which left both of them breathless.

Holly stretched her body on top of his and whispered, "We need to talk."

"Okay, give me a minute," Ethan replied, flipping her over playfully so he could face her. Holly cleared her throat.

"Ethan, I didn't know you and Zahir were brothers."

"Okay," Ethan replied casually. Holly was confused by his reaction.

"I know, but I wanted to hear how you know my brother and if you had a romantic relationship with him," Ethan said, watching her closely.

Holly sat up. "Ethan, I'm going to tell you the whole story. If, by the end of it, you don't want anything to do with me, that's fine - I can handle it."

Ethan watched as Holly tried to explain herself, asking questions until he was satisfied. He smiled as she eventually nodded off to sleep, still looking as silly as she had while trying to explain everything. Ethan already knew most of the details, but this time, he wasn't going to lose to his brother. He couldn't let Holly know that, though.

Zahir and Ethan had been at odds for years and were unable to find common ground.

As Holly slept, Ethan leaned over and whispered, "Will you marry me?"

Chapter 10: Brothers' Gamesmanship

Ethan planned an elaborate wedding and asked his brother to be his best man. Zahir had never had children, but he wanted to have them with Holly. The brothers agreed that if anything ever happened to either of them, the other would love and care for her. Ethan and Holly shared a love that all her friends envied, and even Ethan's friends, on several occasions, tried to break their relationship. However, this only brought them closer.

Holly took a business trip to Dubai, but she fell ill and had to return earlier than planned. When she saw her doctor, she learned she had just lost a child… a child she didn't even know she was carrying. She asked the doctor if she could still have children, and the doctor recommended In Vitro Fertilization. Holly shared this with Ethan, wanting to give him something special, even if it meant risking her own life.

When Ethan heard his wife's plan, he was excited but also angry, as he had promised Zahir that Holly would serve as a surrogate for his brother. Both Ethan and Zahir had used the same family doctor and had donated sperm to carry on the family heir. Now, Holly was pregnant, but she began to feel unwell and had asked the doctor to keep her illness confidential.

During her four-month check-up, Holly discovered she was carrying quadruplets. She was deeply upset, as she had never planned on having so many children. She withdrew from others, overwhelmed by the thought of raising four babies in addition to her two grown, married children. Ethan tried to counsel her, particularly for the sake of her health and the babies.

"Ethan, I feel like a damn rabbit, hatching so many children." Holly's frustration was clear, but Ethan couldn't bring himself to tell her that she might be carrying two different offspring. He wanted to confess but failed. Holly was now in the final stages of her second trimester. She had lost her beauty; her belly was enormous, her feet were swollen, and her face had grown round and puffy. Communication between them had dwindled to holding hands and exchanging the occasional kiss. Ethan began to worry as Holly entered her third trimester.

He decided it was time to tell her the truth. But when he finally broke the news, Holly reacted immediately. She stormed out of the house, holding her massive belly with both hands. She tried to run but failed miserably. The weight of her belly was too much, and the babies were kicking and moving. She sat down to catch her breath, inhaling and exhaling deeply. The thought of carrying so many babies - and the question of who the father or fathers could be - made her nauseous.

Suddenly, Holly began to laugh hysterically and got up, but missed a step and crashed to the ground like an elephant. Pain shot through her body as she lay there, struggling to catch her breath. She clutched her belly and felt the babies kicking and moving. The thought of carrying so many children dazed her, but she didn't call for help. She stayed there and wrestled with the pain and fear.

***

Holly hadn't told Ethan about the fall. The next morning, she was still in discomfort but tried to hide it. Ethan, unaware, kissed her on the cheek. "I've got an emergency meeting today," he said gently. "I'll be back soon." He gave her a warm smile and headed out the door, leaving Holly to cope with the growing pain.

Suddenly, the pain grew even harder. Alone, Holly called for an ambulance, crying and screaming, "Please, please save my children!" She was bleeding heavily, and the first responders rushed to get her to the hospital.

As Holly lay there, she could hear the distant voices of the medics debating whether to deliver the babies and save her life. She was taken straight to the emergency room. The doctors tried everything for a natural delivery, but complications arose, and Holly was no longer responding. She had signed a consent form, which gave the doctors permission to perform a C-section if necessary. With no other options in sight, they proceeded with the cesarean to save both Holly and the babies.

The babies were delivered safely and placed in incubators. Holly, however, was put on life support. The surgeon who performed the operation was excited as this was his first time delivering quadruplets from two different fathers. Holly had given birth to two boys and two girls.

The hospital called Ethan to inform him that his wife was in the hospital. He was shocked, knowing he had only left her at home an hour ago. Rushing to the hospital, Ethan barreled through the halls, pushing past people in his way. "Doctor, is my wife okay?" he demanded.

The doctor shook his head and led Ethan to a private room. He explained that the children were premature but healthy and would need time to develop. "What about my wife?" Ethan asked, sensing something was wrong as he searched the doctor's face. His heart sank.

The doctor told him Holly was in a coma. Apparently, her fall caused complications, and during the delivery, her condition worsened.

"What complications, doctor? Can I see her?" he asked. The doctor told him that he would need to wait a bit. Ethan paced the floor like a restless lion. When he finally reached Holly's bedside, he grabbed her hand and wept uncontrollably. The doctors tried to calm him down, but his sobs grew louder and more desperate.

It felt as though his heart had been ripped from his chest. After several minutes, Ethan's face turned as red as a bell pepper, and his pointed nose became sore from all the sobbing and blowing.

The doctor asked Ethan if he wanted to see his children. Ethan nodded. "Doc, I paid you a fortune… I can't lose both of them. So whatever you do, make sure they get the best treatment."

Ethan called his brother Zahir and shared the news. Zahir immediately took a flight and arrived at the hospital that same day. He, too, stood by the nursery, doing the same as Ethan. The nurses were confused, unsure of who the real husband was, and gossip quickly spread through the ward. Rumors circulated that Holly may have cheated on her husband. Hearing this, Zahir and Ethan reprimanded the staff, resulting in many of the nurses being fired.

The brothers hugged tightly as they walked down the hallway toward the nursery. The atmosphere was eerily quiet, and everyone watched them and whispered. The surgeon accompanied them and explained the babies' condition.

"Doc, how long will they need to be in the incubators?" Ethan asked.

The doctor explained that the premature babies were not yet physically or developmentally ready for the outside world. "They can't regulate their body temperature, they've lost a lot of weight, and their vitals are unstable."

"Doc, are they going to be okay?" both the brothers asked.

The babies were placed in separate rooms, and the brothers hired a nurse for each child. After DNA tests confirmed the truth, it was revealed that both Ethan and Zahir had fathered a boy and a girl each. Meanwhile, Holly was still battling for her life.

The brothers agreed that the children would stay at Ethan's home until Holly recovered, giving her the chance to see them before they were taken away. They took turns visiting Holly and prepared the babies' room, hiring four nannies, who were each fluent in a different language.

Ethan frequently visited the hospital, clinging to the hope that one day he could bring his wife home. Occasionally, the brothers brought the children to see Holly, hoping it would help her wake up. But all their efforts seemed to have failed up till now.

***

A year later, as Ethan was on the brink of losing hope, he sat beside Holly's bed, holding her hand as tears streamed down his face. He begged her to come back to him, sobbing uncontrollably. Then, in desperation, he leaned over and kissed her on the lips.

Holly felt the warm teardrops on her face, and slowly, her fingers began to move. Tears began to roll down her cheeks as well. Ethan was overcome with joy. He frantically called for the doctors, telling them she'd moved.

The doctors rushed in just in time. They had been preparing to take her off life support. They asked Holly to blink her eyes as they asked her questions, praying there was no brain damage.

Rehabilitation was difficult for Holly. There were times when she would give up, staring blankly into the distance. But whenever she heard that Ethan was there, her face would light up. Ethan would kiss her deeply, hold her close, and stay by her side. Zahir and Ethan brought the children for short visits to remind her of the life waiting for her outside the hospital.

Holly's recovery was swift, but the doctors warned Ethan that she might have suffered minor brain damage, so he needed to be gentle with her as they transitioned her back into a home environment. Ethan could hardly wait to be with his wife, and he knew the feeling was mutual based on her reaction when they kissed.

Finally, the day came when the doctors discharged her, and Ethan was there, eager to bring her home. They laughed and talked on the way to the car. They could not wait until they got home. As soon as they reached the car, Ethan set her bag down and gently lifted her chin. Moving closer, he pressed her back against the car, his hand slipping under her dress as he kissed her deeply, trailing his lips down her neck. Holly was overwhelmed with desire. Her body was heating up under his touch.

They quickly flung the car door open and undressed each other in a frenzy. Ethan's car had plenty of space, and the tinted windows provided privacy. In no time, the car rocked back and forth with the intensity of their passion. Holly's moans grew louder, urging Ethan not to stop. Her desire was ablaze, and Ethan couldn't wait to satisfy her. They moved with such vigor that a parking officer knocked on the window. Ethan rolled it down, and the officer, recognizing him, gave a knowing nod and motioned for them to continue. The officer stayed nearby, making sure everything was safe.

When it was over, Ethan stepped out and thanked the officer before driving away. Back home, Zahir had the nannies dress the children, ready to meet their mother. It was a beautiful, emotional moment as Holly, Ethan, Zahir, and the children bonded together as a family.

Later that evening, Ethan had a serious discussion with Zahir about how they would manage the delicate situation of separating the children from Holly without causing harm to them emotionally. Holly, though still upset over the deception, knew she had to face the reality of the situation. She loved Zahir's friendship and agreed to the arrangement that allowed each biological father to care for his own child.

During this time, Zahir's wife remained unaware of Holly and the entire situation. She was more focused on her extravagant lifestyle, spending her weekends partying and getting drunk with friends, which often led to fights with Zahir. Bringing children into such an environment was a recipe for disaster. Fortunately, the mansion was large enough for them to avoid each other for weeks.

Zahir had already prepared a separate room for the children and hired two nannies to help. One day, after not seeing her husband for weeks, Zahir's wife decided to take a stroll around the mansion. The children were playing and running up and down the stairs of the house. As she approached the room, curiosity got the better of her. She began pounding on the door and startled the children, who quickly ran to the nannies.

"Let me in! Let me in right now!" she screamed as her fists hammered against the door. One of the nannies hesitated but eventually opened it, unsure of what was about to unfold.

"What the hell is this? When did we get a nursery? And who the hell do these kids belong to?" Zahir's wife's anger was through the roof.

Right then, Zahir rushed in and tried to calm her down.

"Don't touch me! I said don't touch me!" she screamed, but Zahir still tried to reason with her.

"I don't understand which part of 'don't touch me' you don't get!" she shouted again, even louder. Her fury was like a snowball turning into an avalanche.

Zahir knew he had to find a way to calm her and get her back to their side of the mansion. Finally, he convinced her that the children were there because she couldn't have any of her own. He explained he had arranged for a surrogate mother as a surprise gift.

After a moment of disbelief, she calmed down and reluctantly accepted the explanation. Zahir breathed a sigh of relief. Their anniversary was approaching, so he decided to distract her by taking her on a cruise on his private superyacht without the kids so they could party all night. He even suggested she invite her best friends. This was exactly her kind of thing.

Zahir went all out to please his wife and get her distracted. He hired DJs, caterers, bartenders, lifeguards, etc. The party was set to run from 10 AM until the next day's sunset. Over two hundred guests filled the yacht. Though it wasn't Zahir's style, he thought that pleasing his wife and escaping his own frustrations made it worth it. People danced, drank, smoked, and, of course, indulged in more private activities.

His wife partied so hard she seemed to forget Zahir was even there, spending the night draped over the male dancers with her friends. She drank so much she could barely stand, but Zahir wasn't worried; he knew she was safe. As the night wore on, the guests continued to dance beneath the stars.

At some point, Zahir, exhausted, went to the cabin for a nap and asked one of the security guards to keep an eye on his wife. As the party neared its 24-hour mark, most people were either passed out drunk or still partying. Zahir's wife, however, dragged her friends to the stern of the yacht. There, they laughed and joked until she decided to show off by balancing on the yacht's edge. Her friends begged her to come down, but she continued to balance herself off.

She couldn't swim.

Suddenly, the yacht lurched over a high wave. The lifeguard and security guard tried to catch her, but it all happened too quickly. She lost her balance and fell overboard.

Zahir was jolted awake by the commotion. The lifeguards dove for hours, searching desperately, but they couldn't find her. The U.S. Coast Guard was called in to help. After several more hours of searching, they finally found her body.

Zahir was arrested and charged with her murder. His brother, Ethan, hired the best lawyers to defend him. The legal team gathered evidence, testimonies, and anything they could use to help Zahir. The trial dragged on for months. After days of deliberation, Zahir was finally found not guilty.

During the trial, Ethan took care of Zahir's children. However, the court ruled that Zahir was not fit to care for them, so Ethan continued to look after them while Zahir stayed with him for a while.

But while Zahir was away, Ethan suffered a devastating loss. One of his own children had died. It took a heavy toll on him, and Holly comforted him through it all, pouring her heart into caring for him.

One particular morning, after a long session of passionate lovemaking, Ethan was left breathless. Holly went for a jog and then enjoyed a steamy bath. Ethan watched as she opened the door to the balcony, spread a beach towel on the white bench, and lay down for a sunbath. She was completely nude.

Meanwhile, Zahir opened his own door, which faced Holly's balcony, and saw her lying there. He became so fixated on the sight that he didn't realize Ethan had come up behind him. Ethan placed a hand on Zahir's shoulder. Zahir, not surprised, didn't flinch.

"My brother," Ethan said as both men gazed at Holly. He continued, "I just can't believe how amazing Holly is. She looks younger and more beautiful every day. After so many children, I thought she would've lost it."

Then, he chuckled.

"My love for Holly is like a moth to a flame," Ethan mused while Zahir continued to stare

Chapter 11: The Turning Point

Holly had overheard the conversation between Zahir and Ethan, and it hit her hard. She felt lost like she didn't know who she was anymore. The love she once thought she had for Ethan now felt fragile, broken under the weight of family chaos and endless pressures. Depression slowly crept in, eating away at her confidence and joy.

Ethan, on the other hand, thought everything was perfect. He believed he had the best family - a loving wife who understood him and children who made life complete. But that illusion shattered one day when he came home, and Holly was gone.

What Ethan didn't know was that Holly had been planning to disappear, faking her own kidnapping as a way to escape her life. At the same time, Zahir had his own twisted plans. He wanted to kidnap Holly himself, using her as a weapon to hurt his brother.

Zahir threw a massive party, inviting Holly along. Ethan, busy with meetings, asked one of his guards to take her to the party and promised to join later. Holly and the guard, her driver for the night, were in a carefree mood. But then, the guard's phone rang. Distracted, he reached for it, not seeing the oncoming car speeding toward them.

In an instant, everything changed. The cars collided head-on, spinning wildly off the road and crashing into a ditch. The car burst into flames. The guard died on the spot, but there was no sign of Holly. Authorities searched for days but found no trace of her. Everyone thought she was gone forever.

Everyone except her daughter, Paula.

Years passed, but Paula refused to give up. She traveled to every place her mother had once dreamed of visiting, hoping to find a clue. Each trip ended in disappointment. No one had seen her. Still, Paula kept searching, driven by the hope that one day, she'd find her mom alive.

Then, one day, while on vacation with her husband, Paula decided to take a walk along the beach. The sea was calm and the waves were gently rolling onto the shore. It was a peaceful afternoon, but something strange caught her attention. Sitting alone on a concrete bench was a woman. Her back was facing Paula, and she was gazing out at the ocean. Her silver hair glowed in the sun, and she held a notebook, jotting down something as if she were in deep thought.

There was something familiar about her.

Paula's heart started racing. She knew this woman. She knew it was her mom. But after all these years, could it really be? Nervously, she walked closer. Her mind raced with thoughts of how to approach her. Should she run and hug her? Should she scream her name?

Paula finally built up the courage to speak. "Mom?" she said quietly.

The woman turned to her slowly, with a soft smile, but her eyes looked distant. "Yes?" she asked politely. "Who are you?"

Paula felt her heart drop. It was like a punch to the gut. "It's me, Paula… your daughter," she replied in a shaky voice.

But Holly didn't react the way Paula hoped. She looked puzzled and tilted her head slightly. "I'm sorry," she said gently. "I don't remember you."

Paula's heart broke, but she didn't give up.

"Can I sit with you?" Paula asked. Holly looked at the book in her hand as if someone was disturbing her but then tapped on the empty space beside her.

Paula quickly sat down beside Holly, determined to help her mom remember. "Mom, how are you?" she asked.

"I am your Mom!?" Holly asked.

"Yes, Mom. Don't you remember me? I am your first daughter," Paula said.

Holly wanted to know more from this stranger sitting beside her. "I am your mother-" Holly said.

Before she could complete the sentence, Paula interjected. "Yes, Mom! Yes, Mom!"

Holly insisted that this stranger tell her more about whom she is. Paula did her best to draw her memory. "Mom, do you remember the time you bought a chocolate cake and ate almost all of it? You told us it was burnt and tasted bad, and we believed you! You even said you'd take it back to the store, making such a face we couldn't stop laughing."

For a moment, Holly's eyes lit up. She chuckled, then laughed harder. Tears came to her eyes as she held her stomach. "Did I really do that?" she asked, still giggling.

Paula smiled, nodding. "Yes, you did, Mom."

But then, just as quickly, Holly's laughter faded. Her face turned serious again. "That's funny, but... I don't know you. My name is Holly, but I don't think you're my daughter."

Paula's heart ached. She had found her mom, but Holly's mind was lost in some faraway place. Still, Paula stayed calm. She gently convinced Holly to come with her, to take a trip home, hoping that maybe being in familiar surroundings would help bring her memory back.

As they walked away from the beach, Paula held on to the hope that even though her mom didn't remember her now, one day she would.

On the way, they talked and laughed. Paula felt like she was on the right path but didn't tell her sister Samantha that she had found their mother. When they arrived, Paula pulled into the driveway. Holly was excited to meet new people. As she stepped inside, she looked around and said, "Oh, you have such an elegant home. You must be very wealthy!"

Holly kept wandering around, admiring everything, complimenting Paula's exquisite taste. Paula smiled and said, "Actually, I designed the interior myself."

Holly looked at her blankly. At some point during their conversation, bits and pieces started to come back to Holly, but not quickly enough for Paula. Paula brought out a photo album and said, "Mom, this is when you were a teacher."

Holly looked at the picture and replied, "I was a teacher? Oh no, my child, I've done nothing - no achievements, no accomplishments. I'm just a simple woman passing through life. A failure." Paula ignored her mother's words.

"Mom, here are your sisters," Paula continued.

Holly giggled and said in a mocking voice, "I have sisters?"

Paula went on, showing her more pictures. "This is you on your wedding day," she said, pointing to another photo. Holly just smirked, and Paula, with tears in her eyes, asked if she remembered any of it. Holly pretended to recall, mostly for the children's sake.

As Holly tried to adjust to her new life, the children began taking her out, introducing her to places and people she used to know. Holly struggled to remember, but she tried. Spring came, and everyone was excited to go see the cherry blossoms. Holly thought to herself, "What if things change again? Will I go back to where I came from?"

Paula, meanwhile, waited to see if Holly would slip up, say something wrong, or reveal that her memories were confused due to Alzheimer's. She was trying to see how far her mother could go with her limited recollection. But something didn't sit right. Paula started doing a background check and, to her shock, discovered that this woman wasn't Holly at all - she was Holly's twin sister.

Paula found a note sewn into the lining of a velvet dress in the woman's suitcase. It was a script written by her real mother, Holly:

"I, Holly, shall return to my family with a burst of festive flair! Twinkle. As the embodiment of positivity and resilience, I will tell tales of my adventures in the realm of winter. To my daughter Paula, I remember the day the snowflakes began to fall. I visited your college, and it turned into a winter wonderland. The winds howled, the trees creaked, but you and I stood strong together. The cold air stung, but I adapted. In the beauty of the snow, darkness threatened to take me. Fierce storms raged, and the roads became impassable. But when the snow cleared, I stood tall - unbroken, unshaken. I embraced the white blanket, got in my car, and returned home."

Now, Paula was sure - the woman they had been trying to help remember was not their mother. She took the letter to her sister, and they began to wonder what had happened between their family members. After some deep investigation, they learned from their grandmother that when she gave birth, one of the babies went missing. With limited resources, they had given up hope, but they always believed that the child might come back, especially if she ever needed something from her birth family.

Their grandmother also mentioned that her best friend was pregnant at the same time but had suddenly moved away after giving birth. She further stated that she tried to contact her friend so that she could meet their daughter. Three years later, someone sent a photo of the friend at the park, with a note saying her daughter was having a great time. Eventually, she found out where they were living, and to her surprise, her friend's daughter had the same name as her missing baby. However, nothing could be done because she didn't have the resources to travel.